Floating Solo

Floating Solo

SHELLEY WILSON

HILLFIELD
PUBLISHING

For Jane, Nikki, Karen, Cirian,
and all my romance loving friends!
I'm sorry you had to wait ten years to read one of my novels. I
make no promises that another romance will follow, so make the
most of this one!

Chapter One

Kat stepped from the bow of the narrowboat and slipped the rope over the mooring stake in one fluid movement. After four years of navigating the beautiful Warwickshire canals, she took every action on autopilot.

"Thanks, Kat." The latest guest to enjoy the hospitality of the *Creaky Cauldron* jumped onto the towpath with a slight skip, dropping her rucksack at her feet. "That was the best holiday I've had in a long time," she gushed, pulling Kat in for a tight hug. "I can't wait to tell all my single friends about you."

Kat laughed and squeezed her disembarking tenant back. Since launching Floating Solo, she had welcomed hundreds of singletons on board her floating home for a much-needed, often therapeutic, and sometimes emotional solo holiday.

"If you'd told me I'd be smiling, laughing, and optimistic about my future a week ago I would have told you to sod off." Her guest broke into her thoughts as they prepared to say their goodbyes. "Thank you for everything, Kat. It's been exactly what I needed to help me start over."

"It's my pleasure." Although she hated it when her guests left her, she felt good knowing they were heading off with positive vibes and happy memories. "Let's take a Polaroid selfie for my rogues' gallery."

The large noticeboard in the *Creaky Cauldron*'s kitchen was plastered with photographs of all her Floating Solo guests. The sea of happy, smiling faces warmed her heart whenever she stopped to look at them. Women who didn't think they could ever do anything on their own again until she taught them how to embrace that alone time, enjoy a quiet life, and be comfortable in their own skin.

She had felt the same once. Lonely, disempowered, and scared. Buying a narrowboat was probably the biggest and most insane decision she had ever made, but the thought of being alone in a bedsit somewhere in the city didn't fill her with joy. She craved the outdoors, and the water called to her, even when she was a child. It was her happy place where she would take a walk down the towpaths and wave at the narrowboats as they drifted by. Her father had brought her to the marina most weekends to watch the boats and chat with the owners. The memories she had of those days prompted her decision to buy the *Creaky Cauldron* in the first place, and it made her feel like her father was always with her.

Kat's bubbly guest bounded up the towpath towards the parking area where she had left her car and life behind a week ago. It was a humbling experience to watch her visitors stride off with such determination, especially as a week before she had watched that same person nervously inch towards the boat with hunched shoulders and a grey pallor.

"Another happy customer?" Stephanie strolled up to

stand beside Kat and extended her slender arm to wave the guest off as she tooted her car horn.

"She was lovely," Kat said, reaching down to secure the ropes with a final tug. "Her girlfriend dumped her on their two-year anniversary, and she told me she was sick of wallowing and needed a change of scene. Yesterday, she told me she's moving back to Devon to live with her mum and help her run the teashop they own."

"That's nice," Stephanie said, leaning her back against the boat and lifting her face to the early morning sun. "The magic of the *Creaky Cauldron* strikes again."

Kat laughed and playfully thumped her best friend on the arm. "It's not magic. It's having someone listen to you and not be judgemental."

"Talking of being judgemental, haven't you got your meeting with Paul's investment firm today?"

Kat stopped what she was doing and took a deep breath. Buying the narrowboat and starting her Floating Solo business had given her life hope and meaning. With Stephanie's help she had put together a business plan that involved buying a fleet of boats and hiring other singletons to run the solo holidays in the same way she had for the past four years. Without the proper funding it was just a lofty aspiration, but now the dream could become a reality – if her boyfriend's firm could invest.

"Paul is arranging an appointment with his colleague at two o'clock today. I've got to take the business plan and figures with me, but I also want to take a few photographs from the selfie wall as I think these pictures and what they represent is my unique selling point."

"They'd be fools not to invest in this, Kat. You're changing lives over here, and those photographs show how many people you and the *Creaky Cauldron* help."

"I'm not sure they'll see the emotional element of it. Even Paul's been a bit off lately when I've talked about my plans." She joined Stephanie and leaned back against the boat as the sun shone on both their faces. The breeze blew tendrils of her dark hair across her eyes, and she brushed them away absentmindedly. "He's been a bit off in general, to be honest. I talked about buying a small cottage so I could run the business from land, but he didn't seem too impressed."

"I thought that's what he wanted, to have you grounded and at his beck and call instead of swanning around the waterways." Stephanie winked across at her friend as she teased her. "He was the one who put the idea in your head in the first place, wasn't he?"

Kat nodded, watching a flock of geese squawk across the sky above them. Their hurried flight was in stark contrast to the whispers of clouds that floated in the opposite direction.

"He hinted at me being available for a full-time relationship if I lived on land rather than the part-time relationship we have now."

Stephanie pushed off from the boat and stretched her arms above her head. "I, for one, think your relationship is genius," she said. "Who doesn't want a boyfriend that you only get to see once every few weeks when your boat comes in to moor?"

"I wonder what Tom would say about that. Where you go, he follows."

Her friend's laughter carried across the marina, surprising the ducks that huddled in the shade of the *Creaky Cauldron*'s hull, and Kat couldn't help but smile. Stephanie was partly right; having a part-time boyfriend allowed her to continue living her solo life, which suited her business and the customers she helped, but there was a small part of her that dreamt of walking down the aisle, buying a home together, and having children.

"Let me get through the meeting first," Kat said. "Then I'll deal with the boyfriend drama."

★ ★ ★

"What do you mean it's inappropriate?" Kat stared into Paul's handsome face as he barred the door to his offices, forcing her to express her concerns on the crowded pavement.

"It's a cardinal rule that you shouldn't mix business with pleasure," he said, taking her elbow and steering her further away from the Harper Tyson Group entrance. "Getting my colleagues to look over my girlfriend's scribbled notes is not professional."

Kat took a step back as if someone had slapped her hard across the cheek, and snatched her arm away from his touch.

"Do you honestly think I'd turn up to an investment meeting with dog-eared receipts, a stack of scribbled-on napkins, and a few grand ideas?" She could feel herself getting hotter and more irritated by the moment. Her hands were sweating as she clutched the large manila envelope she had brought along, which contained the carefully crafted business plan she and Stephanie had spent hours putting together. "I'm a businesswoman, Paul, and you promised to arrange a meeting on my behalf."

"There's no need to raise your voice, Kat," he said, moving her further back and into the shade and seclusion of a cluster of trees. "I'll be honest with you. I didn't make the appointment because I didn't believe you'd go through with it."

"You're an asshole!"

An older couple walking their dog startled at Kat's heated words before hurrying on their way. Paul half raised his hand by way of apology and herded her towards an alley on the other side of the trees.

"Please, Kat. I love that you love the *Creaky Cauldron*, but buying more old boats and running a holiday rental for desperate single people isn't the kind of investment HT are going to back. I was trying to spare you from hearing the hard truth."

"Desperate single people." Rage swept over her like a tsunami. "Is that what you thought of me when we met? Do you think you were my knight in shining armour saving me from myself?" She took another step away from him and shook her head to try and clear her swirling thoughts. The betrayal was forcing memories of another time and place to the forefront. A similar conversation where her then fiancé was telling her it was all for her own good. "The holidays I offer are a lifeline to some of my guests," she continued. Her voice sounded hard as she swallowed the lump lodged in her throat. "They learn how to start healing themselves, be comfortable in their own company, develop new skills, and not depend on others to complete them."

"Yes, yes, I know all the hippy stuff, you've told me before, but my firm isn't the right fit. Maybe you could start a GoFundMe campaign or something."

Kat stuffed the manila envelope back into her oversized bag and stalked away; her blood boiled the more she listened to Paul's excuses, and she didn't want him to see how devastating this news was. She had pinned her hopes on getting solid investment from a reputable company that saw her business venture in a positive light.

"Kat, wait!" Paul caught her arm and tugged her to a stop alongside the pop-up coffee cart that provided the regular commuters from the nearby train station with their early morning caffeine. The smell of roasted coffee beans and sweet syrup filled the air as Kat studied Paul's face and waited for him to speak. His hazel eyes had always seemed so exotic to her, but now as she stared at him she could only see a simple man in a cheap suit with no passion or drive for anything that truly mattered.

"There's something else we need to talk about," he said, his shoulders slumping slightly as he huddled closer to her. "I know this probably isn't the best time, but I think it's best if we take a break for a while."

The hiss of the nearby coffee machine mingled with the rhythm of everyone's shoes slapping on the pavement, the cacophony of noises dancing around in her brain. She could hear the birds chirping in the cluster of trees, eager to snatch any crumbs from the sloppy passers-by, and the distant sound of a train pulling out of the station. Tiny fragments of the world came flooding back to fill her senses as she processed what Paul was saying.

"Are you breaking up with me?"

He didn't look directly at her, instead choosing to glance left and right as if he were about to cross a busy road.

"I'm sorry, Kat, but it's just not working. I'm so busy with work that I can't commit to anything else at the moment, and you're always away on that boat."

Kat tried to swallow the huge lump that had risen in her throat, but it appeared to be wedged in tight. The hot prickle of tears spurred her into action and she took a step back from Paul, leaving a large gap on the pavement. Office workers tsked as they had to walk into the road to get around them

"I was trying to find a way to be here more so we could build a better relationship," she said. "But I guess you've managed to destroy all my dreams in one day."

"That wasn't my intention, Kat. I care about you, but I need some space right now. I'm sorry."

He turned his back and hurried through the doors of the Harper Tyson Group, disappearing into the blur of navy suits.

★ ★ ★

The gentle rocking of the boat couldn't soothe Kat's troubled mind. She had watched Paul walk away from her in a personal and professional capacity, taking her dreams of settling down, buying a cottage, and building her business along with him.

"What are you going to do?" Stephanie asked, sipping a glass of wine as they perched on the well deck of the *Creaky Cauldron* under the setting sun. "You can't let one man squash your dreams."

"There's nothing I can do! He never even made the appointment, so I can't go behind his back and rearrange it, because nobody knew I was coming."

"Kat, you need to think bigger than Paul. You need to think about your end goal." Stephanie put her empty glass on the floor and rubbed her palms down her jeans as if preparing herself for an arm-wrestling match. "All you've ever wanted to do was grow this business. It's been your dream for so long. Being a timid singleton is what drove you to buy this beautiful boat in the first place, so don't you dare let someone else take that dream away from you."

As a health and wellbeing coach, Stephanie motivated hordes of women to live the life they wanted and deserved. She had inspired Kat by going after what she wanted and not stopping until she had achieved it. They met each other in a yoga class as two young twenty-somethings and formed a bond that had never broken. Stephanie's mantra in life was to dream it, live it, and become it, and she had made it her mission to help Kat understand the power behind living that way.

Right now, Kat wasn't sure any affirmation, essential oil, meditation, or motivational Tedx talk would ever inspire her again.

"Paul does have more experience when it comes to

making investments; maybe he's right. Maybe Floating Solo is a one-woman, one-boat kind of deal and I'm deluding myself by thinking I've discovered this year's newest craze."

"Bullshit!" Stephanie said with a grand flick of her wrist. "He's not the only investor in the country, so we just need to find someone else for you to meet with."

Kat wrinkled her nose and leaned over the bow to trail her fingertips across the water. It was a simple gesture that always calmed her down. Her father had always done the same whenever they sat along the riverbank, his big fingers disturbing the smooth surface and making ripples that reached as far as the opposite bank.

"Maybe." She shrugged. "We'll see."

Stephanie jumped to her feet and the boat bumped against the side from the sudden movement.

"Oh no, you're not doing that." She placed her delicate hands on her hips. "You're not going to give your power away. Not again."

Stephanie had stood by Kat's side through all her highs and lows. To say she had felt broken more times than Madonna had reinvented herself would be an understatement. Recalling the memories of her losses still triggered strong emotions, and Paul's candid revelations had done nothing to help.

"Look, I love running my business from the *Creaky Cauldron*, so it's not like I'm getting a raw deal. I make a comfortable living, meet some incredible people, have fun, embrace my freedom, and live by my own rules. I can't grumble." Although her words were true, an edge in her voice still betrayed her disappointment. "Besides, if I did find an investor, then my workload would increase, and I'd need employees to run the other boats, plus there would be more marketing to do, and more time on the canals." She lifted her fingers from the water and drained the last of her wine. "Paul's right; it was nothing but a pipe dream."

Stephanie sat on the bench next to her friend and slipped her arm around her shoulder. The sun had vanished beyond the horizon, leaving the hazy glow of fading yellow in its wake.

"But, Kat," she said softly, "a woman without a dream is like a boat without water."

Chapter Two

T he mist hung over the water like a scene from a horror movie as Kat stepped off the boat the next morning. She had wallowed the previous night, not helped by the bottle of wine she and Stephanie shared to commiserate the news Paul had tactlessly delivered.

Her head ached when she first awoke, which reminded her why she wasn't a big drinker. Fresh air was what she craved, and she knew it would soothe her woes.

This was Kat's favourite time of day. The other boat owners were still tucked up in their bunks, and the dog walkers had not yet taken to the footpaths. The birds chirped in the branches high above her head as she set off at a gentle stroll, taking the path that swung away from the marina and up the hill to Mapleton village.

It had become a daily ritual whenever she returned to her mooring. An early morning walk to clear her head followed by a latte and a bacon roll in the village café that doubled up as the local community grocery store.

That day was slightly different from the rest, however. Five years before she had received the news that would change her life forever. Every anniversary was as hard as the previous one, but she refused to spend the day cooped up in the *Creaky Cauldron*, no matter how much she loved the sanctuary of her floating home. Her father would have wanted so much for her to live her life and have fun.

She followed the path as it rose sharply and cut through the open green fields, pausing at the top of the hill to take in the view. Stretching as far as she could see were fields, treetops, and the terracotta tiles of cottages dotted in amongst the woodland. Horses nibbled at grass shoots on a nearby hilltop. A layer of early morning mist that had yet to dissipate camouflaged the marina and the long expanse of canal snaked off into the distance.

She breathed deeply through her nose and exhaled through her mouth, as Stephanie had taught her. Once, twice, three times. The ache in her head lessened and the weight of emotion crushing her chest eased a fraction.

If Stephanie were standing on the hilltop with her, she would say, *Be in the moment. Breathe, rest, reflect, and then crack on with your day*.

Reflecting on what had happened in twenty-four hours was enough to make Kat crack, full stop.

It was hard to think that when she moored up at the marina the previous morning to deliver her latest guest home safely, her life had been about to change all over again.

Stephanie had spent another hour trying to convince Kat that her dream of a fleet of boats was a good idea. She refused to let Paul's limited thinking shake her belief in Kat's plans.

It had felt far too overwhelming to discuss the night before, especially with a few glasses of wine in her, and Stephanie appeared to sense that, when Kat's answers began to consist of one or two grunts. She had kissed her friend's forehead and climbed off the boat to jog the short stretch home to the third-storey apartment she shared with Tom.

The thought of getting other investors involved had seemed so out of reach and daunting. Her safety net was Paul and his influence and support. The lack of both had rattled her more than she wanted to admit to herself or Stephanie.

The gate leading to the main road stood ajar and she tutted to herself at the incompetence of some people. Ensuring the countryside gates were always closed behind you was a rule her father had drummed into her from a young age. They would trek through muddy fields of cows and sheep on their way to visit the boats, and he would regale her with tales of country roads grinding to a halt as a herd of cows escaped their field through an open gate. Her young eyes would grow wide as he told her how businessmen in their big cars would toot their car horns, but the cows refused to move.

The road was empty as she tugged the gate shut behind her. The crunch of the loose gravel beneath her shoes amplified in the early morning silence. There was no traffic on the main road yet. The business community living outside the city would be flicking on their espresso machines and preparing for the commute.

Kat ambled down the hill towards the local store and bakery. In the distance she could see Roger putting up his chalkboard outside the door and crouching to write the day's specials in his usual cursive writing.

"Morning, Kat." He waved as he spotted her approach. "The usual?"

Kat nodded and followed him through the open door. Roger's village store was the only shop in ten miles, so he filled every square inch of the space with everything from groceries to fishing tackle, books to DIY tools, and anything he thought the local community and passing tourists might want or need. It was a treasure trove, and you could easily spend half a day searching the shelves and coming away with an odd assortment of goods.

They walked to the back of the shop where Roger had added a lean-to conservatory for his bakery and café. Over the years, it had become a hub for local residents to meet up for tea and cake and talk about the townies who passed through on their way to the city.

Kat had slipped under that townie radar as the locals embraced her arrival and adopted her as one of their own. That was her father's doing. He had been a regular visitor to the marina and Roger's store and made a point of donating funds to help fix the village hall roof as well as sponsoring the Village in Bloom campaign. Although their family home had been just over the border, her father embraced Mapleton village life. That respect and admiration was something he passed on to his daughter, who loved being a part of such a wonderful community.

"How's business?" Roger asked as he poured coffee into a big mug with a picture of a highland cow on the side.

"It's good," Kat said with a smile. "I returned yesterday with another happy customer. She's going to tell all her friends about Floating Solo."

"That's great, Kat. You deserve all the success in the world. It's been a hard five years for you."

He placed the cup in front of her and put his big gnarled hand over hers. "I know today will be tough, but remember you've got friends here if you need them."

She swallowed down the sudden lump that had lodged itself in her throat and smiled up at the kindly old gent who reminded her so much of her father with his wispy grey hair, bright blue eyes, and warm manner.

"Thanks, Roger. I appreciate that."

He nodded and turned back to add the bacon to the now sizzling pan, letting Kat process her emotions and compose herself once more.

"How are your plans for world domination coming along?" He half turned to ask the question but remained focused on his task. He knew just how Kat liked her bacon and nothing would distract him from getting it spot on.

"World domination might be on hold for the foreseeable future." Kat stirred her coffee slightly too vigorously and sploshed the liquid across the countertop. "My advisor and potential investor turned out to be a fraud in every way possible."

Roger placed a brightly patterned plate in front of her with a large bacon roll steaming in the centre. He shook the tomato ketchup bottle and placed it next to the plate with a grunt.

"You can never trust a townie, Kat."

She half smiled as she tucked into the sumptuous sandwich and lost herself for a moment in the first taste of salty goodness, butter, and homemade bread.

"Can't you find anyone else to invest?" Roger asked. "What about doing one of those fund a crowd things?"

Kat chuckled. "You mean crowdfunding?"

"Yes, that's the one. Surely your satisfied customers are a big enough crowd to help raise the money you need."

"It's definitely something to think about." In truth, Kat didn't think it was the right approach, and putting a crowdfunding campaign together made her head ache all over again, but she valued Roger's support. She was about to suggest he make a list of all his ideas when the tiny bell above the door tinkled.

The noise level rose sharply as two white-haired ladies in velour tracksuits and rolled-up yoga mats barrelled into the store.

"Roger! Roger! Tell Barbara what you saw over at Pete Myers' farm last week; she doesn't believe me. Oh, hello, Kathryn, dear. How are you?" Dotty didn't stop to find out; instead, she bustled up to the counter, dropping her yoga mat on the floor and ushering Barbara forward.

Kat sat back and watched as Roger squirmed under their collective stare. He looked like a youngster who had been caught doing something he shouldn't, and Kat chuckled to herself.

"I told you that in *confidence*," Roger hissed as he grabbed a tea towel and began vigorously polishing a tray of glasses.

"Pfft. You know Barbara wouldn't tell a soul."

Roger's wide, pleading eyes swept to Kat, prompting her to finish off her bacon roll and jump from her stool, excusing herself. She could feel Roger's eyes focusing on the back of her head as she wandered down the aisle towards the milk. Once those ladies were in full flow there was no stopping them, and Kat knew better than to get in the middle.

She tuned out the whispers as Roger, under duress, regaled Barbara with his gossip, no doubt juicy if Dotty was so invested, and concentrated on her shopping.

With a bottle of milk in hand, an avocado, and a bag of mixed vegetables, Kat returned to the counter to pay. Roger had moved on to stories about manure and the cost of petrol as she handed over her goods.

"Isn't this your boat?" Dotty brandished one of the national newspapers in her hand and waved it under Kat's nose. A colour picture of the *Creaky Cauldron* filled half the page under the headline FLOATING SOLO INSPIRES AUTHOR.

Kat snatched the paper from Dotty and laid it flat on the counter so everyone could see. They all leaned in closer to stare at the article.

"That photo was taken last year," Kat said, scrunching up her nose as if that would help the memory surface. "The guest was a freelance journalist from London who was blocked because she'd lost a big client. She wanted a break from all the hustle and bustle and ended up being inspired to write a book."

"Well, it looks like she got on with it." Barbara tapped the photograph lower down the page, taken at a book signing.

"That's fantastic." Kat was genuinely happy. Knowing her boating holidays could inspire people to fulfil their creative goals warmed her soul.

"It says here that she found her muse on the waterways of Warwickshire. Blimey, we'll have townies descending on Mapleton village all summer now." Dotty tutted and nudged Kat aside to sit at the counter.

"Do you really think so?" Roger asked, his smile widening.

"If that article attracts them to the village, you might have loads of extra customers," Kat said.

"Maybe I should get some stationery in. You know how those writerly types love a good notebook."

Kat chuckled as Roger began jotting down a list of items he wanted to add to the already groaning shelves.

"I can't believe she mentioned the *Creaky Cauldron* so much in the article," Kat said, and then, as an afterthought, added, "I wonder if I'm in the book."

"Doubt it," Barbara said. "It's one of those dystopian tales. You know, the ones where everyone dresses in rags and mumbles about the great war. Unless your boat is base camp, I doubt you'll get a look-in."

"It doesn't matter. I'm still delighted she could use her trip as creative inspiration. It makes all the tough days a little easier to cope with."

Dotty rose from her seat and slipped a velour-clad arm around Kat's shoulder. "Tough days? Whatever is the matter, Kathryn, dear?"

"Oh, it's nothing, honestly. I'm feeling a bit low, that's all."

Roger coughed, and Dotty and Barbara glanced at him with that far-from-subtle nod of understanding that their generation was famous for. Sometimes, it was nice that everyone knew your backstory and personal business, as it meant you could offer a simple shrug and be fully understood. One look, one shrug, or a quiet whisper and the entire village went into protective parent mode, which she sometimes needed as a thirty-something orphan. Of course, there were many moments when Kat wished her neighbours didn't know everything about her, but today, she was glad.

"We're all here for you, Kathryn. The kettle is always on if you ever want to pop in for a chat with your aunty Dotty."

Roger half coughed, half laughed again, and reached for his tea towel as Kat fixed a pleasant and appreciative smile on her face.

"That's so kind of you. I'll keep it in mind." The last thing anyone in the village would or should do was pop in for a chat with Dotty. Within hours your name and business would be talked about across the county.

"Can I take a copy of this newspaper with my shopping, Roger?" she said, quickly changing the subject. "It'll be nice to add the article to my photo board."

Roger slid the paper into her bag with the milk and vegetables and slipped from behind the counter to open the shop door. "You'll let me know if you hear of any bus tours heading this way, won't you? I want to make sure I'm fully stocked."

Kat laughed at the twinkle in his eye. Dotty and Barbara might prefer to keep Mapleton village a secret from the outside world, but Roger was a true entrepreneur and if he could smell a sale, he was happy.

"You'll be the first to know." Kat smiled at him.

"Your dad would be so proud of you, Kat," he said in a whisper as she left the store.

"Thanks, Roger; that means a lot."

On the walk back to the marina, she took a detour to the old watermill, which had been converted into apartments about ten years before. Stephanie and her boyfriend, Tom, had moved in about four years earlier and turned the third-floor space into a spiritual sanctuary. You couldn't help but feel Zen whenever you visited.

"Omigod, have you seen the newspaper?" Stephanie screamed as she opened the door for Kat. "It's amazing. Paul must be smashing his head against the nearest wall by now."

Kat laughed and allowed herself to be pulled into a warm embrace. Sandalwood and patchouli scents wafted down the hallway, and the soft tinkling of bells from Stephanie's wind chimes filled the air. She was still in her navy blue pyjamas, which were covered in tiny silver stars, and she looked like the night sky jumping around the hallway.

"What's Paul got to do with anything?"

"Yesterday, he told you Floating Solo was nothing but a hobby," Stephanie said, gripping Kat's shoulders and gently shaking. "Today, your boat is in glorious colour in a national newspaper"

"It doesn't change anything. The article is all about the success of one of my guests. It won't make any difference to Paul or his investment firm."

Stephanie's hands dropped to her side as she shook

her head. "Oh, Kat, you really do need to start seeing the opportunities in front of you."

Tom sauntered out of the bedroom in sleep shorts and sliders, his hair standing in tufts as he rubbed his eyes and scratched his chin simultaneously.

"Morning, Kat." He gave a little wave before disappearing into the bathroom.

Kat grunted a hello in his direction before sidestepping Stephanie and heading for the small kitchen. She scooped the avocado from her shopping bag and placed it on the counter.

"Your breakfast is served," she said with a chuckle.

"Listen, I'm serious. You need to make the most of this exposure. Paul might not believe in you, but we do, and you'd be a fool not to capitalise on this."

"I wouldn't know where to start," Kat said, shrugging. "I've got an Instagram account and a newsletter for anyone interested in life on the water, but I'm no influencer."

"It's fine, we'll help you. Tom does loads of social media content for the estate agents even though it's not in his job description. I'm always joking that he could start a side hustle as a marketing manager."

"Do you think it would help?"

Stephanie beamed and nudged Kat down the hall and into the living room as Tom wandered out of the bathroom.

"Tom will help you with everything," Stephanie gushed, pointing in his direction.

"What am I helping you with?" Tom asked, sitting on the arm of the sofa, looking confused and still half asleep.

"We've got to use this—" Stephanie waved the

newspaper in the air "—to boost Kat's profile and make her the only holiday choice for singletons everywhere."

Tom nodded and scratched his chin. "Yeah, we can do that."

Kat could feel the walls of resistance begin to crumble around her slowly.

Stephanie grinned. "Before you can say River Severn, we'll have Floating Solo well and truly on the social media map."

Chapter Three

Soil spilt out of the small flowerpot and landed on the roof of the narrowboat, prompting Kat to sweep it off onto the towpath. She loved pottering with the small selection of plants and flowers that decorated the *Creaky Cauldron*, but today she needed a distraction more than ever.

Paul had been in touch to arrange a meeting. Not the business meeting she had originally wanted, which would have filled her with delayed joy, but a *we-need-to-talk* meeting, no doubt to clarify the multiple bombshells he had left her with on their last encounter a week ago.

The water lapped against the boat's hull as Kat pressed the earth tightly around the roots of her new basil bush. She had the beginnings of a decent herb garden up here and made a mental note to create a few signature dishes that used her own produce.

"It's looking good, Kat."

Paul's deep voice cut into Kat's culinary musings. Even though she knew he was coming, the sight of him still stirred a mixture of emotions. He had left his suit behind and wore dark jeans and a woollen navy jumper which hugged his muscular frame.

He had hurt her a lot, but she couldn't deny the

attraction she still felt for him. Had he changed his mind and acted hastily when he asked for a break?

They had been together for three years, navigating their peculiar relationship between her Floating Solo business and his busy career and social life. He lived for playing golf and spending time with his golfing buddies, which often only left a few small windows of time for dating and romance, but they made it work – or so she thought.

"I like what you've done with the bow," he said, gesturing towards the colourful assortment of scatter cushions and throws she had added to the seating area.

"Tom suggested I add a few more homely touches for the Instagram reels. He said people like to imagine themselves in a space. It speaks to their emotional brain, apparently."

Paul nodded as if he was fully on board with Tom's marketing strategy.

"The videos are great," he said, reaching over to steady the boat as it bounced in the wake of another passing narrowboat. "I can see how a home-from-home environment would appeal."

Kat suppressed a snort as she studied his face. He seemed genuine, but in all the years they had been together, he had avoided going on any boating trips with her, preferring a boutique bed and breakfast.

"One of Tom's many bright ideas," she said, rearranging the herb pots so they were more aesthetically pleasing – another suggestion from Tom. "He thought it might attract any single people who are looking for an escape but struggle to leave the comfort of their homes."

Kat didn't wait for a response. She stood up and dusted down her soil-covered jeans before heading to the bow. Paul mirrored her along the towpath until they were face to face.

"Are you coming aboard?" She motioned for him to sit on her newly spruced-up benches and began shifting the cushions to make more room.

They sat together in silence for a while, watching a couple of boats drift past and waving at any dog walkers who ambled along the towpath, until Kat thought she might burst from the awkward anticipation.

"What is it you need to talk about?" She knew. He'd blurted out that he wanted a break and she hadn't chased after him. Despite wanting to call, she had remained stoic and given him the space he had asked for. They hadn't spoken for seven days. He might still yearn for a single life, but a man like Paul couldn't rest without some emotional outburst and begging. It was good for his ego.

"I wanted to check you were okay," he said, tilting his head to one side in that universal show of sympathy. "I hadn't heard from you."

"You told me I wasn't good enough for your business and then followed that bombshell by telling me I wasn't good enough for you either. What exactly did you expect?"

Kat took some small pleasure from the slight flinch to Paul's shoulders. Had he honestly thought she would want to speak to him in a civil manner after what he had said and done?

"Bit harsh," he mumbled, looking out over the water and avoiding eye contact. "I thought we had always valued honesty in this relationship. I wanted to tell you how I felt."

"But you didn't, Paul. You didn't tell me anything besides your need for space, which is ironic as *space* is something we both have plenty of thanks to my boat clients." Kat's voice hitched slightly at the end, and she took a deep breath. She had promised herself she wouldn't get upset, but whenever she thought back to that day a week earlier outside the Harper Taylor offices, the swell of disappointment rose from deep in her gut.

"I thought we would be planning for our future and looking for a home together. Instead, you push me aside, tell me my business is nothing but a silly idea and now you wonder why I'm not a sobbing mess."

He opened his mouth to answer, but Kat cut him off as she continued her rant; her disappointment was beginning to manifest into rage that built the more she looked at him. "Well, I'm sorry to disappoint you, but I'm sick of giving my power away to men who don't believe in me or support my dreams."

"You sound like Stephanie," Paul said as his top lip curled into a snarl. "It's got nothing to do with that hippy shit. I do believe in you. If I didn't, I wouldn't let you swan around the waterways with any old crazy person."

"Let me! Let me! Get the hell off my boat, Paul."

Paul's face drained of colour as he realised his error.

"I'm sorry, Kat. I didn't mean it like that. You know me…"

"Unfortunately, I do. Maybe you were right all along, and we are so different that we don't belong together. I trusted you to stand alongside me as I built my business, but you've shown me that I'm very much alone in that respect."

Paul scrambled back onto the towpath and backed away from the *Creaky Cauldron* as if Kat might start flinging plant pots at his head at any minute.

"I don't want to lose you, Kat," he said. "I know it sounds stupid after telling you I want a break, but my head is all over the place, and I don't know what else to do."

"Leaving me alone for a while is a good place to start," Kat said, her anger dissipating slightly. She cared deeply for him, which is why his actions hurt so much, but not having him in her life would hurt more. "I've got a busy season coming up, so maybe we could talk again after that when we've both had time to cool off and think."

He smiled and shuffled back a few steps. "Okay, that sounds good. We'll take a break and catch up in a few weeks."

Was that relief on his face? Kat shrugged and spun to rearrange the scatter cushions. Anything to distract herself from what she truly wanted to yell at him. Was he even aware of how much he had hurt her? Couldn't he see how, in one simple conversation, he had all but shattered her dreams? Kat heard his footsteps retreating down the path and sucked in a ragged breath. The tears she had been holding on to spilt over and tumbled down her cheeks. She was annoyed at herself for getting upset, but she equally allowed herself this moment to grieve the potential end of something.

In her heart, she knew she wanted to reconcile, but her head was telling her something different. He had shown her what mattered most; her aspirations weren't part of that. She wanted someone who respected her business savvy, supported her ventures, and loved her unconditionally, but she doubted that a man with those qualities existed.

With one last look at Paul's broad shoulders disappearing into the marina car park, Kat returned to her pots and the quiet calm of her herb garden.

★ ★ ★

"The last reel got over a thousand likes," Tom said as Kat stirred the big pot of vegetable curry bubbling away on the hob.

"Is that good?"

Stephanie laughed and poured the wine. "Yes, that's good, Kat. The more likes, comments, and engagement, the more people learn about the *Creaky Cauldron*."

"You're getting lots of comments," Tom added, holding his phone aloft as if Kat could pick out the text from across the galley kitchen. "We could do a Q and A-style video where you answer the most-asked questions. People love that behind-the-scenes stuff."

"I'm not sure about being on video. Who wants to see my pale face when they can watch the beautiful countryside instead?"

Stephanie bustled around, setting down the cutlery while shooing Tom away from the breakfast bar.

"I don't think you realise how gorgeous you are, Kat. Everyone would be drooling over their phones watching videos of you and this boat, don't you think so, Tom?"

Tom's gaze never left his screen. "I refuse to answer that in case it's a trick question and you're trying to get me to admit your best friend is hot."

Kat laughed as Stephanie rolled her eyes. "See, Tom thinks you're gorgeous too."

"I'm not sure. Maybe we could ease into me being the online face of Floating Solo. I'd much prefer the *Creaky Cauldron* was the star of the show."

All talk of Instagram content, videos, and engagement statistics was put on hold as the three friends ate. It had become a regular date night whenever Kat was back at the marina. She cooked, Stephanie brought the wine, and Tom usually provided the entertainment with wild stories of his house viewings.

The evening's storytelling extravaganza included a naked lover who got caught climbing out of the spare room window when Tom arrived to show the house to a sweet old couple looking to downsize.

He laughed. "I'm not sure that's the kind of downsizing they were expecting."

"Did they put in an offer?" Kat asked.

"Yes, and the old dear asked if the naked man came with the fixtures and fittings."

They laughed and opened another bottle. Kat curled up in her favourite armchair and watched her friends snuggle together on the small sofa, giggling like teenagers. She loved spending her time like this. The biggest appeal of running her Floating Solo business was her interaction with everyone who travelled with her. Each customer would flop into that sofa and share their life story. Kat was a host, cook, sailor, and counsellor, but she adored every second.

Her dad had been a good listener and was often caught up in the village by strangers who would open up about something important. They would look bewildered for a moment as if they had no control over the words pouring from their mouths, but then her dad would impart his wisdom, inspire them to rethink their woes, and send them away with a spring in their step.

Kat often felt like her father was with her on board the *Creaky Cauldron*, still watching over her and channelling his good listening skills into her. Being able to listen to people's problems and challenges and find a positive thread to pull on was a gift Kat appreciated. It was one of many skills her dad had taught her.

Stephanie broke into her thoughts. "We wondered if you wanted to join us."

"Huh? Sorry, I was daydreaming. What did you say?"

"We're going to the Crick Boat Show at the weekend to take some video footage for your social media. Tom thinks it will be good to show other boats and then flip back to the cosiness of the *Creaky Cauldron*. It's a bit like, you've tried the rest, now try the best."

"I love it. Count me in. I've got a three-night trip this week, but I'll be back in Mapleton by Friday morning."

"Perfect. It's going to be fun, and maybe you could look at other boats to invest in when you expand the business." Stephanie winked as she said this.

Kat was thankful that her friend was so invested in expanding Floating Solo even though she knew how deflated Kat was about Paul's refusal to take her business idea to his firm.

"Hmm, we'll see."

"Yes! See, I knew you'd come around once that prick was out of the picture."

Kat hadn't told Stephanie all the details of her chat with Paul, or that their separation could be temporary. To be honest, she wasn't sure how to tell her friend. In fact, she wasn't sure how to process it for herself. In her head, she felt their relationship was over, as he had rejected her in the most hurtful of ways, and yet her heart was still clinging to the smallest of hopes and that dream of settling down.

"Let's focus on getting the *Creaky Cauldron* on everyone's radar before we start buying a fleet of boats." Kat laughed. Yes, she still felt jaded, but she didn't want to push aside the dream of expanding just yet.

★ ★ ★

"If you ask me, that boy doesn't realise what he's lost." Roger was stacking tins of beans on the already crowded shelf as Kat absentmindedly read the label on a tin of vegetable soup.

"He's an idiot for not investing and an even bigger fool for letting you go," Roger continued. "Who doesn't see the potential in expansion?"

Roger's store had expanded in a variety of ways. First were the wall-to-ceiling shelving racks allowing for more stock lines. Next was the conservatory-come-café-come-bakery that doubled as a community hub. Finally, there was a one-bedroom holiday flat above the shop that Roger rented out to the influx of tourists who flocked to the area. Being in the heart of Warwickshire, and in particular, a stone's throw from Shakespeare's hometown, meant a steady stream of visitors. Roger's love of expansion was driven by his need to provide what his customers wanted. Something Kat could relate to.

"I guess Paul doesn't have the same business brain as us," Kat said, picking up a small plastic bucket and spade from the floor and setting them aside. Listening to the rain hammering against the conservatory roof made her briefly question the need for buckets and spades, not to mention the lack of sandy beaches in the local area.

"Townies for you." Roger laughed. "They swan around in their company cars wearing suit trousers that don't reach their ankles and think they know it all. Tsk, they wouldn't know a good deal if it bit them on the…"

The tiny bell above the door tinkled and Roger's head spun in that direction.

"Be right with you," he called out before handing the half-opened box of beans to Kat.

Without prompting, she carried on stocking the shelf as Roger bustled off to serve the new customer. The quiet hum of conversation in the background washed over her as she continued her task. Her thoughts automatically drifted back to Paul and his failure to see what she was trying to achieve. Roger understood. He could picture Kat's vision and even appreciate the backstory that prompted every thought and idea. Why couldn't Paul?

Part of her wondered what she had done wrong, but

the other part of her, the strong independent part, knew this wasn't on her. Stephanie was always telling her to stop giving her power away, but Kat hadn't fully understood what her friend meant until now.

Before her father died, Kat had been engaged to a successful, handsome, funny, and sociable man. She thought he was the one until he broke it off two weeks before the wedding. Shattered, Kat had moved back home. Hiding away in a small village was the only way she could cope. Her father welcomed her and was her rock as she navigated her emotions, shed a million tears, and wallowed in her anger and mistrust. She knew it was her dad that got her through that rough patch, but when he died a month later, only then did Kat experience true devastation.

Maybe everything happening in her life was the universe testing her to check she wasn't letting her standards slip. Either that or she really did have dreadful taste in men.

Apart from her dad, and Roger, she was starting to wonder if there was another man in the world worthy of her trust, respect, and love.

The bell tinkled, signalling that the shop was again empty of customers, and Kat wandered to the counter, handing over the now empty cardboard box.

"So, what's the plan?" Roger asked, wiping down the counter.

"Vegetable soup for dinner and a good book," Kat said with a smile.

Roger rolled his eyes and flung the cloth at Kat's head. "I meant with the big dream."

"For tonight, curled up with a bowl of soup and a good book is the only dream that matters. Tomorrow, I'll worry about what comes next."

"Fair enough, but remember you're a savvy businesswoman who deserves success. Your dad wouldn't want you moping around after that suit and putting your plans on hold."

Kat smiled at her friend. Roger had known her dad well and had been there for her when he passed away. If anyone had her back, it was him.

"I'm regrouping, that's all. With Tom's marketing help and you and Stephanie supporting me, it'll all work out."

"That's the spirit. Now, do you want some fresh bread to go with that soup?"

Chapter Four

The Crick Boat Show was a huge success. The trio wandered through the show village as Tom captured video footage of Kat chatting with the exhibitors, fellow enthusiasts, industry experts, and more. She drew the line at him filming her stuffing her face with ice cream, although Stephanie was happy to oblige.

The quayside was packed with exhibitors and excited visitors, and it gave Kat a buzz to see how many people enjoyed life on the waterways.

As they ambled down to the marina, Kat stopped to check on the Crick Boat Show Favourites. Shiny awards were being handed out to the best in show, and she was delighted to see the boat builder who lovingly made the *Creaky Cauldron* scoop another prize.

"You should put yourself forward to run the boat-handling taster courses next year, Kat. That would be a great way to promote Floating Solo at this event."

"That could be fun."

There was so much potential, and Kat's head was bursting with ideas as they drove back home from Northamptonshire. The show had been exactly what she needed to prove to herself that her venture was worth pursuing.

The girls had left Tom sifting through all the photographs and videos he had taken to grab something for dinner, as they were all famished after the long drive home.

"I'm not being biased," Stephanie said as they trudged up the stairs to the apartment she shared with Tom, "but the *Creaky Cauldron* is the best boat in the world. It's got a real home-from-home atmosphere about it that those other boats can't pull off."

Kat chuckled. "And the fact you love it so much has nothing to do with the fact your best friend lives on board?"

"I said I wasn't biased." Stephanie laughed. "Okay, maybe I am a little bit, but I also think it's the fact you live on board that gives you the edge. The boats we saw for hire today were modern and functional but had no real heart. What solo travellers want is to feel like they're in a safe space, and you create that for them."

Kat smiled as she followed Stephanie up the stairs. She adored living on the *Creaky Cauldron* and how simple life could be. There was no mortgage to pay and no noisy neighbours. Apart from dry-docking the boat every two years for hull blacking and paying insurance and river permits, living on the water was affordable and fun.

As they reached the landing, Tom burst through the door, brandishing his phone and falling over his words.

"What the hell?" Stephanie stopped mid-walk, causing Kat to bump into the back of her.

"You will *not* believe what just landed in your DMs, Kat." Tom was slightly flushed, and his usually ruffled hair seemed to be standing to attention as if it were also excited by whatever had Tom so hyped.

"Breathe," Stephanie said in the calming work voice she usually reserved for her yoga students. "Let's get inside, and then you can tell us what's got you bouncing off the walls."

The door had barely clicked shut behind them when Tom blurted out his news.

"An agent has been in touch to see if Kat would be interested in filming a two-week Floating Solo holiday-style documentary with a high-profile celebrity!" Tom's wide eyes and smile were accompanied by sweet, if somewhat uncoordinated, jazz hands.

Stephanie's high-pitched squeal made Kat jump.

"Omigod! That's amazing. They must have seen your new-look Instagram account and all the positive engagement. Kat, this is huge."

"How high-profile?" Kat asked, trying to quell the nervous churning in the pit of her stomach. "Are we talking a low-level Z-lister or Taylor Swift?"

Tom stretched his arms wide and took a deep breath. He looked like he was about to burst into song.

"It's Jordan fucking Harrington!"

Stephanie's squeals went supersonic at that point, and Kat had to lower herself into the nearest chair before she slid to the floor in shock.

The world knew Jordan Harrington as a big Hollywood celebrity famed for his many action-hero roles and high-profile, if somewhat volatile, relationships. His latest girlfriend was Lexi Chivers, the sweetheart of Netflix's number-one serial drama. Kat couldn't deny she was a big fan, but the thought of such a person spending two weeks on her narrowboat didn't make any sense.

"What did the agent say?" she said, trying to get her jumbled thoughts in order.

"Her name's Martha, and she's working with director Ted Hawkins and a small team on a docuseries in which they take big stars and put them in ordinary situations. She says in her message that the collaboration would be good for them, good for you, and good for business."

"Oh, Kat, this is it. This is the big break you need. Forget Paul's investment firm. You've got Hollywood backing you now, baby."

Stephanie and Tom danced around the small living space, and Kat couldn't help but laugh at their exuberance. Until she saw the message for herself and did a bit of digging into its authenticity, she was going to remain grounded. She knew Tom had been working hard to build on the publicity from the newspaper article, but a Hollywood star wanting to navigate the River Avon befuddled her brain too much to focus.

"Have you replied to the message?" she asked, suddenly fearful that in his excitement, Tom had signed her up without talking it through first.

"Not yet. I thought you'd want to do that."

"Do it now," Stephanie gushed. "With the time difference, you'd be better off messaging her straightaway; otherwise, if you wait until the morning, it'll be the middle of the night for her and you might miss the opportunity."

Tom thrust his phone into Kat's hand, and she trembled as she opened the message and read everything Martha had written. It was matter of fact, which calmed Kat down, as she could ask questions and hopefully stall deciding for another day or two.

'Dear Martha, thank you for your interest in my Floating Solo holiday experience. I'm intrigued by your request and would welcome a chat to discuss the details further. Yours sincerely, Kathryn Sinclair.'

Stephanie and Tom exchanged a look.

"What?" Kat asked. "It's a perfectly professional response. I refuse to get all fangirl-y over a direct message."

"I wasn't expecting you to fangirl, but a bit of warmth and humour might be nice."

Before Kat could respond to her friend, the phone pinged, and Martha's name popped up in bold at the top of the screen.

"She's answered already. Blimey, she's keen." Tom chuckled, waving his hand at Kat to open the message.

'Hello, Kathryn, thank you for your quick response. As I mentioned in my previous message, our director, Tom Howard, wants to film a docuseries with Mr Harrington. The idea is to film Jordan's experiences as a normal guest. We want to include footage of him doing everything you do with your other guests, such as driving, cooking, parking, etc. We are hoping to include footage of local establishments so that it would be beneficial to your local community. Is this something you could accommodate? What are your thoughts? Regards, Martha.'

"Driving, cooking, and parking!" Tom laughed. "Well, Martha, Kat's initial thought is to include a training day so she can teach you the lingo."

Kat giggled. While it was true that driving and parking had no place on the canal, it was common for her guests to know nothing about narrowboats, life on the water, or the terminology and etiquette that went with it. She did, however, like the idea of a training day.

Without hesitation, Kat tapped out her reply.

'Thank you for the clarification, I'm confident I can accommodate all your needs. To get a fully immersive experience with the highest chance of capturing the right footage, I recommend a fourteen-night trip around the River Avon with an additional set-up day to teach you and your crew how to steer, operate, and moor the boats safely. The Creaky Cauldron *sleeps two, so depending on the size of your crew, I will need to hire additional boats. Does this sound acceptable? I'm happy to have a chat over Zoom or Teams with you and Mr Howard if you have questions. Yours sincerely, Kathryn Sinclair.'*

"Woah, Kat, that's a great response," Stephanie said, reading the message over her shoulder. "I knew you'd have a fleet of boats once you believed in yourself again. You've manifested exactly what you deserve."

Did Kat truly believe in herself or even think she deserved success, or was she responding out of some morbid curiosity? The thought of pushing her Floating Solo business into the spotlight thrilled her, but Paul's words still swirled around her head. Now they had broken up, however temporary, she was once again one of the desperate single people he had callously referred to.

'That all sounds perfect, Kathryn. Thank you. I'll liaise with Ted and send over some dates when we can have a call to finalise the details. Regards, Martha.'

Martha's message flashed up on the screen and the heat began to sweep through Kat's body. It was happening.

A Hollywood A-lister was going to be joining her on a fortnight's jaunt through Warwickshire. If she said it out loud, she doubted it would sound real.

"Looks like I'm going to need to find another boat," Kat said finally.

Tom and Stephanie began dancing again, leaving Kat to deal with the tsunami of thoughts that battered her brain. There were far too many what-ifs about this trip, but if they ironed out the details before they left, then maybe, just maybe, this could be the start of something special.

★ ★ ★

"Would I know this Jordan Harrington fella?" Roger asked as he smothered Kat's toast in butter and slid the plate across the counter.

"Have you watched *Rogue Sniper?*" Judging by the creases littering Roger's forehead, he hadn't.

"I'm more of a good old Western fan than any of that loud action nonsense," he said. "Give me Clint Eastwood or John Wayne any day. Now those fellas could act."

An image of Roger sitting in front of his television wearing a Stetson pushed its way to the front of her mind, and she stifled a giggle.

"I don't think Jordan Harrington has ever done a Western or a romance, come to think of it. He always seems to be cast in explosive films with lots of gunfire and fast cars."

"Well, I'm sure a couple of weeks on the canal is just what the he needs then. Life moves fast enough without having to create films that make it move even faster."

Roger had a point. Kat couldn't remember the last time she watched a film that wasn't loud, brash, and bloody. She momentarily wondered why Jordan Harrington had never been cast in a romcom or one of these feel-good Christmas love stories that she and Stephanie binged every winter.

There was no denying the man was gorgeous. He was tall, lean, handsome, and had an adorable crease in the corner of his mouth when he smiled. Kat had watched most of his movies over the years and absentmindedly followed the stream of relationships he had via the glossy magazines at the hairdresser's. Would she call herself a fan? Probably not, but if there was a quiz about Jordan's likes and dislikes, Kat would win. She made a mental note not to bring that up in conversation when Jordan and the team arrived.

"Is the other boat at the marina yet?" Roger asked, interrupting Kat's daydreaming about Jordan's love of freshly ground coffee.

"Not yet. Blake should be delivering it this afternoon. It's got an open-plan galley and four single berths, so it's perfect for Martha's crew. She told me it would be her and Ted, then Cole and Beth, who would be doing camera, lights, make-up, and wardrobe."

"Does that mean Jordan will be sharing with you?"

Kat had been overwhelmed when Martha and Ted told her about the sleeping arrangements. Even though the *Creaky Cauldron* had two double berths, there was still only a thin partition wall separating her bedroom from Jordan's room. Ninety-nine point nine per cent of Kat's guests had been women, with the exception of a sweet old widower whom she couldn't turn away. Sharing her home with a strange man gave her a peculiar sense of unease, and the only reason she agreed was because of who that man was and because an entire film crew would be in the boat behind them.

The whole project felt surreal. Once they arrived, Kat hoped that she would get so caught up in work mode that she would forget the high-profile passengers and start to enjoy the trip. It had been a long time since she had been away for longer than a week, and she was looking forward to sharing some of her favourite bars, restaurants, and independent shops on the route with her American guests.

"Yes, the director wants it to be as natural and realistic as possible, so they're going to instal a couple of small cameras in the galley to capture the mundane tasks of making a coffee in the morning, eating at the breakfast bar, playing board games and all that."

"Board games. Do these Hollywood stars play board games?"

"I've got no idea," Kat said with a laugh. "Maybe there's a celebrity Monopoly club we don't know about."

They laughed at the idea before Roger bustled off to find Kat's order. When they had finalised the trip over Zoom, Kat had wanted to ensure there were a few special touches to make Jordan and his team feel as comfortable as possible. She had asked Roger to source her a couple of retro coffee grinders, decent cafetières, and some good quality, fresh coffee beans.

The small touches were always what her Floating

Solo guests noticed the most. Whether it was adding their favourite foods and drinks for the trip, a hot water bottle, the personalised slippers she left in their room, or the gorgeous Molton Brown toiletries she stocked in the bathroom, every detail was thoughtfully considered.

Most of the positive reviews referred to Kat going above and beyond, but for her, it was an easy way to make her guests comfortable and to get to know them better. She always sent out a form asking for any allergies and intolerances, their shoe size, likes and dislikes, and anything else she thought would make a difference to their trip.

Martha had filled out the form on Jordan's behalf, although everything listed Kat had already read about in *Cosmopolitan*. She didn't, however, know that his favourite coffee roast came from Mexico. Enter Roger and his incredible knack for getting hold of anything from anywhere.

"Here you go, Kat."

Roger dropped the box onto the counter and opened it with scissors. Kat stood to peer into the open box and get a better look at the goodies inside. There were two retro-style coffee grinders in deep mahogany wood with a tiny winder and a cute little drawer where the coffee grounds collected. The smell of coffee wafted out of the box, and Kat could almost visualise Jordan's smile when he took that first sip.

There were four bags of coffee beans, as Kat didn't want to leave the crew out and had doubled up on everything. Two glass cafetières sat at the bottom, wrapped heavily in bubble wrap.

"They're going to love this. Thanks, Roger."

"Anytime. If this docuseries attracts more American tourists, I might start stocking this stuff regularly."

Kat did not doubt that if anyone would benefit from her impending guests, it would be Roger and his store.

Keeping busy with these finer details was the only way Kat knew to stop the whirling sensation in the pit of her stomach that had been ever-present since Tom told her about Martha's message. It all still felt unreal, and she couldn't erase the feeling that at any moment she would wake up and realise there was no Jordan Harrington, no potential fleet of boats, and no chance of a real future.

With all the preparation for this trip and rearranging some of her other guests, Kat realised she hadn't had time to think about Paul. It felt good to be able to focus on the positives rather than the tumultuous on-again, off-again relationship. Although she thought he might have sent at least one text message after Martha's team shared the news of them being her next guests. Who was she kidding? The only people she could rely on were her closest friends, who supported her through the highs and the lows.

Her Instagram account continued to flourish under Tom's supervision, and this small success had created a side hustle for him that brought in more money and amazing connections, which pleased Stephanie.

Seeing her friends thriving made Kat happy.

"Do you want me to drop this at the marina when I do my deliveries?" Roger asked, packing the coffee beans back into the box.

"That would be great, thanks. I need to pop in and

see Stephanie before heading back to the boat. She's been feeling rough for a couple of days, and I want to check on her before the chaos begins."

"Send her my love and these." Roger handed her a small bunch of flowers from the bucket by the till. "I hope they cheer her up."

Kat knew they would and thanked him before heading back up the hill towards the old watermill. She stopped by the weir to watch the swirling water as it hit the lower level. The recent rainfall increased the river's ferocity as it toppled over the top. In the distance, swans floated majestically, oblivious to the roar of the water.

This was one of Kat's favourite spots in Mapleton village. The stone bridge gave the perfect vantage point from which to watch the weir and the wildlife. When she was a youngster, her father would bring her to this bridge, sit her on the stone ledge with his big hands holding her tight, and tell her about the many creatures that inhabited the riverbank. He would point out the butterflies, bees, coots, herons, and dragonflies, and they would make up stories and adventures that the birds and mammals would have.

She wiped away a tear and resumed her journey to Stephanie's. Now wasn't the time to reminisce about her dad. There was work to be done before Hollywood arrived and shattered the peace and quiet of Mapleton village.

As she reached her friend's apartment, her mobile rang and Blake's number flashed up on the screen.

"Kat, I'm so sorry." He sounded flustered. "The boat I've booked out for your trip hasn't got back yet. The family who hired it before you have run into the bank, and we've had to send a rescue team to retrieve them. I can't be sure if there's any damage until I get it back to the boatyard, but it means I'm going to be a day late getting you your other boat."

Kat's chest grew tight at the thought of her VIP clients arriving with nowhere to sleep. There was no way she would fit six people into the *Creaky Cauldron*.

"And you haven't got anything else that would work?"

"I've got nothing left, Kat. That article in the newspaper about your boat has been great for my hire business, but it means all my other boats are out on rentals."

She tugged absentmindedly at the hem of her jacket as a million thoughts and potential scenarios bombarded her brain.

"Don't worry, Blake. I'll figure something out, but keep me posted."

She shoved her phone back into her pocket and leaned against the wall of the watermill. What the hell was she going to do? This wasn't the first impression she wanted to give Martha and her team, or Jordan Harrington, and there was no way of delaying them as they were already in the air, bound for England.

With sweaty palms and a racing heart Kat ran up the three flights of stairs in the hope that Stephanie wasn't too poorly for some emergency brainstorming and to help her figure out what to do next.

Chapter Five

Kat watched three navy Range Rovers sweep into the marina car park and stop by the gate and the single-track path that led down to the water.

Hollywood had arrived.

At Stephanie's suggestion, Kat had left a message for Martha so she would have a heads-up about the lack of a boat situation when they landed. After she'd rung the local hotels with no luck, Roger stepped in and saved the day by handing over the keys to his one-bed flat above the shop. Kat had to hope and pray that Martha, Ted, Beth, and Cole would be up for sharing the flat as much as they were looking forward to sharing a narrowboat.

Stephanie had insisted that Tom be on site to take a video of their arrival, as she was still feeling under the weather, and demanded that the entire experience be documented in her absence.

"Are you ready for this?" Tom asked, zooming in on the cars as the doors opened.

"Not in the slightest." Kat said with a sly smile. "But when has that ever stopped me?"

Chuckling, they both watched as a distinguished-looking silver fox climbed out of the first car and looked around. He caught sight of Kat and Tom and waved in their direction.

"That's my cue," Kat said, taking a deep breath to steady her nerves. She began walking up the path to meet her new guests, scanning the cars for that first tantalising glimpse at Jordan Harrington.

A pretty lady in her sixties with dark curls and huge sunglasses almost covering her entire face jumped out of the car and began barking instructions to the drivers. In a flurry of activity, the chauffeurs began unloading the equipment and suitcases. Kat recognised Martha from their Zoom call.

Kat watched a young man with shoulder-length hair and bold tattoos climb out of the third car and stretch his arms above his head. He was strikingly handsome, but he wasn't Jordan. When he reached for the camera equipment, Kat realised this must be Cole, the cameraman. Climbing out of the same car, a petite blonde girl stumbled onto the tarmac, shielding her eyes from the early morning sunshine.

Kat was fairly certain Los Angeles was much sunnier than Warwickshire, but she suddenly felt enormous relief that their introduction to narrow boating wasn't in torrential rain.

"Kathryn! Hello, Kathryn!" Martha marched forward with her right hand outstretched and her left hand clutching a well-used notebook.

"Hi, Martha. Please call me Kat. It's lovely to meet you in person. Welcome to Mapleton Marina."

"It's just as quaint as you told me. I love it. Ted, Ted, do you love it?"

Ted sauntered over to where they stood and shook Kat's hand. His face was littered with deep wrinkles that

showed a well-lived life, and when he smiled, it lit up his
entire face. There was something incredibly calming about
Ted Hawkins, and Kat took an instant liking to him. He
wasn't what she expected a big Hollywood director to be
like, but then, she knew nothing about their world. What
the hell should a film director look like?

"You've got a beautiful little boatyard here, miss." His
thick Southern American accent made the entire sentence
sound like something from a romance movie, and Kat had
to consciously stop herself from gawping at him.

"Thank you. The marina is the pride and joy of the
villagers. It attracts lots of boaters, which is great for the
economy, and being so close to Shakespeare's birthplace
means there's plenty to see and do in the area."

"I remember Martha telling me 'bout the link to
Shakespeare. Maybe you could introduce this little ole
group to some culture, and we could catch a play while
we're here."

Kat mentally kicked herself for not thinking of doing
that but vowed to check with the ticket office at the Royal
Shakespeare Theatre as soon as she had them all settled in.

"Are you going to introduce us to the *Creaky Cauldron*?"
Martha crackled with unused energy. In a weird way, it
complemented Ted's calming manner, like he was the
ying to her yang. She walked on the balls of her feet as
if she needed to be ready to sprint at any given moment.
Kat wondered if being an agent meant being on call all
day, every day. Despite the liveliness of Martha's aura, Kat
felt comfortable in her presence. Both she and Ted oozed
confidence and respect.

"Of course, follow me." Kat headed off down the footpath towards the boats like she had done a million times before, and yet today, she felt oddly disconnected, almost like she was watching everything from outside her body. Even though Martha and Ted had explained the need for this docuseries to be as relaxed and as normal as possible, it was as far from normal as Kat had ever been.

"Did you get my message about the crew boat?" Kat glanced sidelong at Martha, who was keeping pace with her. "I can't apologise enough for the delay."

"Oh, honey, don't worry about it. We understand, although I do hope we won't end up crashing any boats on this trip."

Kat laughed with a mix of humour and relief. "Nobody will crash on my watch, I promise. Now, I've managed to secure you all a bed in my friend's flat. It's got one double bed, a couple of blow-up mattresses, and a sofa bed, so I hope that's okay for one night."

"Sounds like the adventure will be starting early," Ted said with a chuckle.

Jordan Harrington still hadn't made his entrance and that worried Kat. What if he was sitting in the blacked-out Range Rover, wondering what he had signed up for? The man was a professional and used to plush trailers and penthouse hotel suites, no doubt with a gold star on the door. A catering, wardrobe, and make-up team followed his every move, making sure he was fed, watered, and looking perfect. What would he think when he saw the tiny toilet in the *Creaky Cauldron* and the equally tiny shower cubicle? For one second, her beautiful narrowboat felt inadequate.

Kat turned her hands over to check that her palms weren't sweating as much as she imagined, but just in case, she wiped them down her jumper as they arrived on the towpath.

"Welcome to the *Creaky Cauldron*," she said, motioning to the colourful seating area at the well deck. "I've been assured that *Dreamcatcher*, which is the four-berth for you and your crew, will arrive tomorrow."

"It's adorable," Martha cooed. "Even better in real life. Your reels are fabulous, but the real thing is better."

Kat felt a swell in her chest on hearing Martha's words. She knew how special the *Creaky Cauldron* was because it was her home, but when other people recognised the magic, it filled her heart with joy.

"I can't take credit for the Instagram reels," Kat said, waving Tom over. "My friend Tom does all the social media marketing. He's the one who makes me look good."

Martha laughed and shook Tom's hand enthusiastically. "You need to speak to Beth; she's going to be doing our behind-the-scenes content, and I think she'd value your expertise and input."

Tom was herded off in the direction of the petite blonde as Cole arrived with the first of the silver equipment cases. He was a handsome and solid man with bulging muscles on his arms, no doubt from manoeuvring the heavy camera equipment around all day. His lopsided smile was full of warmth.

"Is it okay to set up a few small cameras inside?" he asked.

"Of course. Let me show you around and you can decide what's best."

After she warned Cole and Ted about the low doorway at the entrance, they followed her inside and regrouped in the living room. Kat watched both men for any negative reactions but was pleasantly surprised by their look of awe.

"It's so cosy," Cole said. "I can see why people like spending time here. I was expecting it to be a bit cramped, but the space is set out perfectly."

Kat glanced around her home with pride. She had worked so hard to create something functional and beautiful. When she wasn't taking solo travellers on adventures, she was curled up in her favourite chair, reading a book or watching films. The décor she had chosen reflected the tranquil vibe she felt whenever she gazed out at the water and countryside.

The walls were painted a yellowy cream to make the space seem bigger, but it also instantly made you feel warmer when the sun streamed in through the tiny windows. The décor was teamed with the pale blue and grey fabric of the cushions and throws. The built-in shelves were full of books, photo frames, knick-knacks and little ornaments collected from her many travels. Everywhere you looked, there was a story to tell.

The kitchen units were also cream with pale wooden counters and wrought-iron handles shaped like anchors. To ensure she had a more comfortable living space, she had opted for a breakfast bar and high stools instead of the fixed table and chair option that other boats favoured. She loved it when her guests perched on the stools as she cooked dinner. Most of the conversations that mattered happened in that space.

Pretty blue and white storage containers sat beside the kettle, and Kat had set up a fresh coffee station on a tray with the grinder, beans, and cafetière. She saw Ted nod in approval at the small touch.

"As you can see, from the bow, you enter the living space and then move along to the kitchen. You'll find the bathroom behind the first door down the corridor. The first bedroom on your right is where Mr Harrington will sleep. The door facing you at the end leads to my room, and then you'll reach the stern beyond that."

With Kat's approval, Cole set off to explore the space for the best camera angles, leaving Ted to talk to her about the logistics of their trip.

"I'd like to get initial shots of you and Jordan as we set off, with the marina in the background. As an opening scene, it works well, as we can bookend it when we get back at the end of the fortnight."

"I like the sound of that," Kat said, picturing the scene in her mind with the breeze ruffling her hair and Jordan smiling across at her in a retelling of Kate and Leo's epic moment from *Titanic*. She shook her head to dislodge the image. "You can take those shots from a couple of angles. If the crew boat left first, you could film us following you, but you could also set up along the towpath and capture the narrowboat as it passes by."

"If we set up on the towpath, we'd have to leave someone behind," Ted said, an adorable crease appearing between his eyes.

"The boats only travel at four miles per hour, so if Cole was filming from the towpath, we could slow down to pick him up and he could jump back on board. It'll work for your opening scene."

"Who is jumping back on board?" Cole asked, fiddling with a tiny camera.

"You are." Ted and Kat spoke at the same time and then burst out laughing.

"You'll be fine, Cole, I promise. I jump on and off all the time to manage the locks."

"Ah, yes, tell me about the locks," Ted said. "I want to film Jordan doing one of those, as they look fascinating."

Kat chuckled. "He'll have plenty of practice. We'll be travelling on the Avon Ring, which has one hundred and thirty-one locks to navigate."

Cole whistled long and low. "There's no way to avoid them?"

Kat studied Cole's face to see if he was joking, but the deadpan expression told her otherwise. She knew locks were a strange phenomenon to most tourists, but if they were going to get anxious at every hurdle, it would be a long trip.

"No, we can't avoid them. The route we'll take means most of the locks will be at the start of the journey. I won't lie to you; they're hard work, and it's pretty physical, but once you get into a rhythm, you'll be fine. We'll all need to work together on this, so I hope you and your crew understand that it's a hands-on experience." Kat directed the last part at Ted.

In all her marketing materials, she was upfront about how much her guests would be involved in the maintenance and travel. It had never been an issue before. Everyone loved the idea of working the locks and seeing how life on the water really looked – but would her Hollywood guests be the exception?

"It's no problem, Kat. We'll all pitch in when needed, I promise."

Although the words came out of Ted's mouth, his posture told Kat another story. It gnawed at her again that Jordan Harrington hadn't appeared yet. Had Ted and Martha prepared their big star for what he needed to do? Without full cooperation, this trip could turn into a nightmare.

As if sensing her unease, Ted changed the topic and asked Cole about the camera choices.

"It's a tight space for angles, so I think if we put one at the back of the kitchen, one at the entrance, and one in the corner of the living area, we'll cover all the main activities."

Kat was relieved they weren't adding cameras near the bathroom or bedrooms. The thought of turning the *Creaky Cauldron* into some *Big Brother* reality TV show didn't sit well with her. Filming them cooking, chatting, cleaning, and relaxing with a glass of wine over good conversation was acceptable, but nobody needed to see footage of her snoring or running to the loo in the middle of the night.

Through the window, she could see Tom talking to Beth as he showed her his phone. She loved the attention that his hard work was getting. Stephanie would be mortified that she had been absent through all of this. In truth, Kat was missing her friend's support. The entire situation was overwhelming. She was used to dealing with single travellers, not a group. Maybe Paul had been right, and she wasn't cut out for expansion.

Leaving Cole to set up the cameras, she led Ted back onto the well deck and into the bright sunshine. She took a deep breath and let her gaze wander along the surface of the water and along the canal. That view always calmed her nerves, and today was no exception.

"It's beautiful," Ted said softly. "I can see the appeal of living on the water. Where I'm from, we've got big ole lakes, but nothing so intimate."

Kat liked that. Intimate. It was the perfect way to describe the canals. On most of the waterways, you could always reach the towpath or bank, so it felt safe and secure. Although she loved being by the water, large expanses like the ocean or a lake felt different. Perhaps it was also the slow pace that appealed to her. Their trip around the Avon Ring would take two weeks, with about five hours of cruising each day. Would her new Hollywood friends be able to cope? She was about to find out.

In the distance, Kat spotted a tall figure get out of the last Range Rover and adjust his sunglasses. He was on his phone and throwing his free hand in the air in an animated motion. Relief washed over her as she recognised Jordan Harrington. A tiny part of her had begun to think it was all a hoax and Jordan wasn't coming, but here he was.

"Let me introduce you to Jordan," Ted said, extending his hand to help Kat off the boat.

They strolled along the towpath, passing Tom and Beth, who were filming the back of the *Creaky Cauldron* on their phones. Beth waved enthusiastically, and Kat knew instantly that she would enjoy getting to know the young make-up artist. Martha had said something about behind-the-scenes footage, which sounded much more relaxed than the professional filming Cole would be doing. She also added that Beth had the energy and excitement to make it *pop*. Although Kat didn't know what that pop entailed, she guessed it could be fun finding out. She also knew that Stephanie would want her to embrace this entire experience and report back with a British translation of what a behind-the-scenes pop was all about.

Jordan had wandered down the path and was talking to Martha as they approached. He was even more handsome in real life. His dark hair was neatly trimmed into his neck but left longer on top, so it flopped ever so slightly, making anyone in his vicinity with a heartbeat want to reach out and push it back. He wore dark jeans and a navy polo shirt that hugged his muscular frame. Kat thought the glossy magazines hadn't made enough fuss over his jawline as it was all she could focus on as they got closer.

Martha was speaking quietly, but Kat flinched at the sharp tone in Jordan's voice as he snapped at his agent. As a true professional, Martha brushed it off and spun to greet them.

"Jordan, I want you to meet Kathryn Sinclair," she said.

Kat lifted her hand in readiness to shake his but stopped midway when Jordan Harrington ignored her completely and stormed off in the direction of the boat.

Ted rushed after him, throwing an apologetic smile in Kat's direction.

She let her arm swing back to her side as a lump formed in her throat, not because she wanted to burst into tears but because she was forcing herself not to shout abuse after his retreating back. What was that saying again? Never meet your heroes.

"It's been a long trip getting here from LA, and with the unexpected delay, it's left a few niggles in his schedule," Martha said. "He'll return to his old self as soon as the jetlag clears."

Kat almost laughed at Martha's words. How was it possible that she, Ted, Cole, and Beth were all perfectly lovely when they had taken the same trip and were dealing with the same jetlag and delay? Martha had brushed aside the rudeness of a man clearly old enough to know the importance of good manners.

No. It was clear to anyone with eyes in their head.

Jordan Harrington, the big superstar action hero from Hollywood, was an asshole.

Chapter Six

"I can't do this, Steph. He's awful." Kat had managed to slip away to her friend's apartment for an hour as the crew unpacked and set up the equipment on the boat. Roger had given Martha and the team a grand tour of their one-bedroom apartment, and so far, nobody had stomped their feet and demanded a refund.

The idea had been to acquaint themselves with how everything worked that day and then do more training on steering and maintenance before they set off in the morning, but that had to be pushed to the next day once Blake delivered *Dreamcatcher*. All the tension and delay had given Kat indigestion, and she sipped on the chamomile tea Stephanie made her.

"But he's so lovely in interviews and on the red carpet," Stephanie said in a tone that suggested Kat was making it all up.

"I promise you, the red carpet Jordan is nothing like the real-life Jordan. He's an entitled pig with the manners of a spoilt child, and I can't believe that man has to stay with me on my boat for two weeks. Maybe we could cancel the trip."

"Don't you dare. You are making a lot of money from this, enough to start investing in your Floating Solo dreams and turn them into reality. Come on, Kat. Do you want to be alone forever? Expanding the business will allow you to settle down, grow roots on land, and make room for a proper relationship. Okay, so Jordan Harrington is a pig. You've dealt with men like him before. Blimey, you were even engaged to one once."

Stephanie rarely brought up Kat's ex-fiancé unless she needed to make a point. Kat pulled at the hem of her jumper as if still trying to hide behind a shield. Her brow creased and her entire posture shifted as her shoulders slumped. Even after all this time, the thought of the man who had ditched her just before their wedding reduced her to a squirming shell, which was the trump card in Stephanie's argument every time she tried to empower Kat.

"This isn't your usual singleton trip. You've got an entire crew along for the ride. You told me Martha and Beth were nice, so stick with them and only speak to Jordan when you have to. Make it work, Kat."

She knew Stephanie was right – about everything. Most of the days would be taken up with cruising, teaching the crew about life on the water, and filming, and when it came to the evenings, she could tell them about the best local pubs and restaurants and stay behind for some peace and quiet. Maybe she would use that time to map out her goals for her future and update her business plan.

"If I throw him overboard in a rage, I'm blaming you," Kat said with a smile.

Stephanie laughed and squeezed Kat's hand. "You never know; he might grow on you."

"Like a fungus on the hull that'll cost me thousands to fix."

"It's two weeks, that's all. Give him the full *Creaky Cauldron* hospitality, smile for the cameras, and know it'll end soon and you can ship him back to LaLa land."

"Two weeks," Kat repeated. "Two weeks, and then it's back to dealing with nice people with warm smiles and positive vibes."

"Exactly. Besides, I'll need you back here looking after me, because Tom has been so busy that I'm starting to feel like a singleton myself."

Kat felt pangs of guilt as she watched her friend rearrange the cushion behind her back. Tom had been working so hard to help Kat build her visibility online, especially with the high-profile visit, that she hadn't realised how much of his time she had been monopolising.

"I'm sorry. I keep dragging him away from you to do my marketing stuff. Hopefully, this docuseries will generate enough hype that Tom can take a break and be at your beck and call again." Kat hugged her friend, knowing full well that Stephanie also loved her own space.

As if on cue, Tom arrived home with a bag of groceries and a bunch of yellow roses, which he deposited into Stephanie's arms with a tender kiss on her forehead.

"Have you told her?" he said.

Stephanie's brow wrinkled as she shook her head. "No, she's got enough on at the moment."

"Told me what? What's going on?"

"Nothing, honestly; he's talking about me being ill and the fact I'm missing out on the Hollywood action. You know how much I love the limelight."

Kat could tell she was lying. The dark circles beneath

Stephanie's eyes were a sure sign that she wasn't sleeping, which always pointed to an illness. They had told her Stephanie wasn't well at the moment, but was it more serious than they were letting on? The thought of leaving her friend behind and spending two weeks with an asshole didn't make Kat feel any better.

"You know I'm here for you no matter what, don't you? Hollywood hero be damned. If you're sick and need me, you only have to say."

"I'm fine, Kat. I promise. Tom is here to look after me, and if he keeps bringing me beautiful flowers then I might have to marry him one day too."

They all laughed. Stephanie and Tom had never been bothered about marriage. There was no denying that they loved each other and happily created a life together, but they did it without the expense and drama of a wedding day.

"Now I know you're really ill," Kat said with mock horror. "When *you* start talking about marriage, there must be something seriously wrong."

She didn't miss the tiny look that passed between her friends but decided against pushing the matter. They would tell her when they were ready, and in the meantime, she had to entertain a narcissist in her home for a fortnight and needed to be fully focused.

★ ★ ★

Martha, Ted, Cole, and Beth had received the delay with the additional boat reasonably well, but the deep scowl that morphed Jordan's usually handsome face into that of a stroppy teenager made Kat's palms sweat.

He had made it clear that the extra day to the schedule was inconvenient. Correction, he had made it clear to everyone else but within earshot of Kat. Speaking directly to the hired help appeared to be impossible for the big star.

As an apology for the boat's delay, Kat managed to buy last-minute tickets to visit the Royal Shakespeare Company to see *The Merry Wives of Windsor*, Shakespeare's famous comedy.

"I can't tell y'all how excited we are to be seeing a Shakespeare play in the place he was born," Ted said as they all ambled up to the car park and the convoy of Range Rovers Martha had arranged for their night out.

"It's a great play," Kat said, trying not to remember the time Paul had taken her to see it on her birthday a couple of years ago.

"What's it about?" Jordan asked, his tone suggesting she was dragging him kicking and screaming to the theatre rather than it being a pleasant evening of culture and laughter.

Kat didn't pause for a second before shooting back, "It's about lies, jealousy, and dirty laundry." She stopped herself from adding, '*a bit like your last article in* Cosmopolitan*!*'

"Ooh, sounds fun," Beth shouted from behind them.

"It is. And us girls will have the last laugh," Kat said.

She couldn't make out Jordan's mumbled words as he stomped off towards the last car, but she did catch Ted's 'cut it out' comment as they climbed inside.

The theatre was bustling as they arrived, and the small

group received plenty of appreciative glances as Jordan meandered through the foyer. A few of the theatregoers brave enough to approach managed to get a selfie or autograph as they all made their way to the doorway for the upper circle.

"Upper circle? Really? You couldn't get us any further away from the stage?" Jordan raised his eyebrow as Kat handed the usher their tickets.

"It was all very last minute," she said, and then instantly wondered why she was even bothering to explain herself to him. "We were lucky to get any tickets at all."

They filed into their seats, and Kat realised with horror that she was sitting next to Jordan. His long leg pressed up against hers as he squeezed into the small row of seats.

There was no way she could focus on Shakespeare's wit when she was so close to Jordan. In a way she was glad she had already seen the production as her concentration was on everything but the merry wives. By the interval, she was starting to feel a dull ache in her limbs from trying to lean away from him for the last hour.

When the second half got underway, she gave in and allowed her leg to bump Jordan's. As he didn't flinch away in disgust, she was able to settle a little and enjoy the second half.

"Popcorn?" Jordan waved the bag of sweet and salty goodness under her nose, and she gratefully grabbed a small handful.

"Thanks." Maybe there was a glimmer of hope that he was human after all.

★ ★ ★

Dreamcatcher was the same size as the *Creaky Cauldron*, but the interior layout was slightly different. The well deck led straight to the living area, but instead of a comfy sofa and armchair, there was a fitted corner bench seat and a large table.

For the crew, it was more practical as they could use the table to spread out their notes and plan their filming schedule.

From the living space, you entered the galley, with kitchen units on both sides of the narrowboat, making it a corridor style instead of sectioned off like in the *Creaky Cauldron*. The entire interior was wood-panelled with cream curtains and brown carpets.

Kat had known Blake, the owner, for a few years and often signposted enquiries to him when people asked her about hiring a narrowboat for themselves. He was a warm and friendly man who loved the waterways as much as Kat. His fleet of boats was identically decorated inside but had fun names such as *Freedom*, *Hope*, and *Dreamcatcher*.

Looking at the sparse décor, Kat understood better why her own boat appealed a lot more. It made sense to keep everything plain and fuss free when hiring out to strangers, but Kat preferred the personal touches. If she did have her own fleet one day, each boat would be just as quirky as the *Creaky Cauldron*.

"Have you all settled in okay?" Kat stood in the doorway watching Ted and Cole pore over their notes at the table as Martha made a pot of coffee. Beth appeared from the bedroom area with a pile of crisp white towels.

"It's too cute," Beth said with a wide smile. "Have you seen the dinky bunks?"

Kat laughed at her excitement. *Dreamcatcher* was designed specifically for friends, with four single beds split between two bedrooms. In the *Creaky Cauldron*, the two bedrooms were doubles, giving herself and her guests more room to toss and turn in their sleep.

"The bench seat and dining table also turn into another bed if anyone snores too loudly," Kat said. "The extra bedding should be underneath the seat."

"Good to know," Beth said, nodding in Martha's direction.

"I do not snore," Martha said with mock indignation.

The girls laughed as Martha handed Kat a steaming mug of coffee and Beth bustled off to deposit the towels in the bathroom.

"It's an adventure," Martha said, sipping her drink and watching a dog walker on the towpath. "For all of us."

Kat assumed that the last bit was for her benefit, and after the previous night's theatre trip and Jordan's firm dismissal of spending their first night on her boat without the crew close by, *adventure* might not have been the word she would have used to describe what was happening.

"Talking of adventures, are you ready for your first training session? It's time to start honing your helmsmanship skills."

Due to the confined space to the aft of the narrowboat, Kat decided to teach the film crew in twos. Martha and Beth went first, much to Beth's delight. She was in her mid-twenties but behaved like an excitable teenager, which Kat thought was adorable. If Beth could remain so upbeat in such a toxic environment, then she was certainly winning at life.

"There's a lot to think about when navigating a narrowboat down the canal, and I'm going to bombard you with information, so please ask me if you don't understand anything." Kat was in full flow. This was the part of her Floating Solo business that made perfect sense to her. Explaining the rules, etiquette, and processes necessary for a safe trip was normal, and she fell into her comfortable groove. "When you're ready, you'll start the engine and keep it in neutral so it warms up. You'll untie the mooring ropes from the bank, grab any pins, and store them on the boat, as that'll make it easier for you to moor when you stop."

Martha and Beth nodded along in understanding. So far, so good.

Kat continued. "You'll push away from the bank to make it easier on the rudder, but if you're in shallow water, you may need to reverse a bit before changing into forward gear. I'll advise you before we leave each mooring, so don't worry too much."

"Do we need to stick to the left like on your roads?" Beth asked.

"Great question. It's actually the opposite, so you should remember this bit as it'll be like your road system. The rule is to stay on the right, but most of the time you'll be steering down the middle unless another boat comes in the opposite direction. It's shallower near the bank, and we want to avoid getting the rudder tangled in weeds."

Gripping the tiller, she explained the basics of steering. The group hadn't yet decided who would steer *Dreamcatcher*, but as Ted and Cole would be busy directing and filming, it was likely going to fall on one or both of the women's shoulders.

"You steer canal boats by the tiller, which connects to the rudder," Kat explained, pointing over the back of the boat and into the water. "When you push the tiller to the right, the boat will go left, and when you pull the tiller to the left, the boat goes right. Got it?"

She moved out of the way and motioned for Beth to stand to the left of the tiller.

"Get a feel for pushing it away from you and then pulling it towards you. You only need small movements; otherwise, you'll crash into the bank. The important thing to remember is that the boat will take a few seconds to react to your actions. Try to anticipate your moves."

"The boat looks so long from this angle," she squealed. "How long is it?"

"The *Creaky Cauldron* and *Dreamcatcher* are both sixty-two feet, but they're used to this waterway, so don't worry. I'm not getting you to do anything that can't be done."

Martha took Beth's place at the tiller and tried her hand at pushing and pulling.

"You're a natural," Kat said with a smile.

"How do we stop?" Martha asked, looking around the stern for what Kat could only assume was a handbrake.

"Another great question. There are no brakes on a narrowboat, so you need to give yourself plenty of stopping time. Put the boat into neutral and then use your reverse gear to slow down. We'll also have one crew member each to jump on the towpath and brace the rope at a forty-five-degree angle. This will bring the boat to a stop, and then we can tie it off."

"You make it sound so easy, Kat. How on earth do you do all of this on your own?"

"I've had years of practice, and living on board means I'm always using my skills to avoid them getting rusty. My father loved the canals, and I feel close to him when I'm on the water, so I can't imagine doing anything else."

She wasn't sure what prompted her to open up about her father. She was usually the one who became the on-site counsellor listening to other people's stories, but here she was sharing information about her own life.

"I lost both my parents when I was a kid," Martha said softly. "My uncle raised me and still looks out for me now, even though I'm a grown-ass woman."

Kat couldn't imagine anyone looking after Martha. She was an organisational and independent powerhouse, and in the short time Kat had known her, she was already in awe. Stephanie always said you could get a sense of what a person would be like from their written correspondence, and in this case, she was right. Martha had always been professional, polite, and courteous in her emails and text messages, and left Kat feeling at ease. The second she met her on the walkway to the marina, Kat knew she was everything she had hoped.

"My mum raised me all on her own," Beth added. "Pop left her when I was a baby, so it's just been the two of us, but I'm lucky that she's such a strong and independent woman. She taught me how to live my life well."

"Your momma taught you how to live life *too* well." Martha chuckled. "Honestly, Kat, I've never met anyone so young who has done so much."

They laughed as Beth took a mock bow.

"And I'm all yours," she said, blowing a kiss.

Martha rolled her eyes, which made Kat and Beth laugh even louder. It felt good to connect with them both.

"Have mercy on us, Kat. We're going to need all the help you can give us."

"Don't worry. I've got you." Despite the humour, Kat knew the importance of making sure her guests were okay with every aspect of life on the water. "When we set off in the morning, I'll check on you and make sure you're both comfortable steering. Maybe take it in turns so you can build your confidence, but I wouldn't advise you to both be here at the same time as it'll get crowded and one of you will probably end up in the water."

Beth found that hilarious and instantly jumped on her phone to record herself. She held her phone up high to capture herself with Martha standing behind her, still holding onto the tiller.

"Who will get wet first?" she said, speaking directly to the phone. "Will it be contestant number one, agent extraordinaire Martha Collins, or will it be your favourite make-up artist to the stars, Bethany Anderson? Stay tuned for more."

"You guys are crazy," Kat said, laughing.

"It's just a bit of fun, and besides, the behind-the-scenes videos build a lot of buzz for the show. It's like getting famous before you get famous."

"I'm not so sure about the getting famous bit." Kat giggled. "But if you manage to film anyone falling into the canal, make sure it isn't me."

★ ★ ★

Roger swung by to deliver the groceries and essential items for the first leg of their trip and was a huge hit with Martha and Beth. Kat could see Beth's phone camera out as Roger juggled onions on the towpath.

She loved how involved her friends were in this project and hoped it gave them the boost they needed to thrive. Roger and his quirky store deserved an entire show of their own, and no doubt Dotty and Barbara would feature heavily.

What surprised Kat more was the lengthy conversation and laughter Jordan shared with Roger before he headed back to the shop. She was itching to find out what they had talked about. The more she watched Jordan from afar, the more he confused her. His smile was infectious and readily available for anyone who wandered along the towpath and stopped to find out what was going on.

She found herself seeking him out and watching his movements like she was David Attenborough on the hunt for wildcats. Jordan appeared to know the effect he had on people as he brushed any praise aside and acted like lifelong friends with everyone he spoke to, which made Kat feel all the more disappointed that he hadn't turned that smile on her.

As they were planning an early start in the morning, she had suggested dinner on the boat rather than a night at the local pub. Cole had taken some convincing, as he was keen to sample the local ales, but the others were happy with a relaxed evening, good food, a bottle of wine, and getting to know each other. As *Dreamcatcher* had the big table, they decided to eat on the crew boat.

"Does everyone like mushrooms?" Kat asked Ted, who was working on his shot list.

"If there's one thing you'll learn on this trip, Kat, it's how much this crew eat and that nothing is off the menu."

She chuckled as she began slicing the mushrooms and added them to the already sweating onions. "Good to know."

Cooking for her guests was a joy, and over the years, she had mastered a few decent recipes that were quick and easy to prepare and even easier to eat.

Lost in her own thoughts, she didn't see Jordan arrive until he was hovering over her shoulder and staring at the pan in horror.

"You're not cooking, are you?"

Although slightly taken aback by the sharpness of his manner, she tried not to let his spiky attitude invade her personal space. "Yes, I'm making spaghetti bolognese," she said, in a mildly sarcastic tone.

"Can't we order in?"

Kat glanced at him in time to see the smallest hint of a smile. She ignored the quip and carried on with her task. One moment he was sharing his popcorn and the next he was criticising her cooking in jest. Jordan Harrington was a confusing individual.

He disappeared as quickly as he had arrived, leaving the smell of soap and cologne lingering in the air. Kat peeked over her shoulder to where Ted sat. The pen in his hand, which moments ago had been scratching across the page, was now still. He was staring at the empty doorway with sad eyes, and the grooves in his forehead looked deeper than usual.

"So, is everything as you expected?" Kat said, purposefully interrupting Ted's melancholy.

"Yes, yes, it's all great. We're even lucky with your British weather."

"Blimey, now you've done it. Any mention of weather on the open water sets a curse in motion."

"Really!" Ted's face fell until Kat began laughing.

"No, I'm kidding, but don't get your hopes up about the sunshine. I've checked the forecast, and we'll definitely be getting a few spring showers on this trip."

"That's okay. Dark skies and rumbling thunder make for great atmospheric shots. Besides, Martha made us all pack our raincoats to be safe."

Not for the first time, Kat saw Martha and Ted as the parental figures in this small group. It almost felt like she was invading a family holiday. Martha bustled around, constantly on the go, ensuring everyone was in the right place and had exactly what they needed. Kat had seen her drop a baseball cap on Cole's head as he sat in the sunshine fiddling with his camera equipment, and she thrust numerous cups of coffee under Ted's nose as he worked on his storyboard.

"Have you all worked together before?" Kat was

intrigued by the group dynamics. Surely a big movie director would have hundreds of people around him. Although she understood the need to scale down the crew due to the nature of the project, she wondered what Ted had left behind in Hollywood.

"Martha has been Jordan's agent for as long as I can remember, and she's helped co-produce quite a few of my projects," he said, getting a wistful look in his eye. "We've worked on everything together, big and small. She found Jordan modelling in a charity fashion show on a trip to Boston and brought him back to LA with her. I liked the kid, so I cast him in a low-budget movie I was working on. It hit the big screen, and Jordan captured the hearts of audiences worldwide."

Kat remembered reading about Jordan's big break and his chance meeting with a big-name agent. It felt strange now to be able to put a face to the names in that article.

"Cole is my best camera guy and also a brilliant cinematographer and goes where I go. He understands how I work and knows what I need before I do sometimes. And then there's Beth. Martha worked with her on a sitcom a few years ago and liked her energy. She thought she'd be a good fit for Jordan and joined the team about eighteen months ago. We're a quirky bunch, but we make it work."

"I can relate to quirky," Kat said with a smile. "My friends fit that vibe too, so I think we'll all get along great."

After a long pause, Ted added, "I won't apologise for Jordan, but I will ask you to be patient with him."

In any other situation, that statement would have felt wrong, but Kat found herself nodding at Ted in an attempt to prove her loyalty. She was part of his quirky little team now too, so getting on with the job at hand, doing as she was told, and trying to make this trip successful was just as important to her as it was to Ted and Martha.

All she had to do was avoid Jordan Harrington and make it to the end of this fortnight without telling him exactly what she thought of him.

Patience was what Ted needed, and patience was what she was going to try to achieve.

Chapter Seven

The spaghetti bolognese was a big hit, and Kat felt a smug sense of pride when Jordan's eyebrow raised briefly after his first forkful. Everyone cleared their plates, and Cole even asked for seconds.

The wine flowed as quickly as the conversation, but Jordan stayed mostly silent, only adding one or two cutting remarks when the opportunity arose to ridicule someone at the table. The others didn't appear to notice, or they were incredibly good at ignoring the jibes, but Kat's temperature rose with every barbed comment.

It wasn't her place to call him out on it, and she had promised Ted she would be patient, but if every mealtime was like this, it wouldn't be long before she told him what she thought of him to his face.

Watching the group interact was better than any TV show. As a huge fan of *Friends*, Kat knew what good entertainment looked like, and the banter between Ted, Martha, Cole, and Beth was up there with the best. What Kat found more interesting was Jordan's role. In his movies, Jordan was handsome, vibrant, and likeable, but in reality his expressions soured any natural beauty and he could be borderline cruel.

"Are there any actors you didn't enjoy working with?"

Kat asked, jumping into the conversation. She eyeballed Jordan as she spoke but doubted anyone at the table would admit it was him, even if it were true.

"Who was that young wannabe from the UK?" Cole asked. "What was his name? You know, the one who thought he was entitled to everything and demanded we pay his travel expenses?"

"Jason? Jenson? Justin!" Martha shouted with a laugh. "He was straight out of acting school and thought the world owed him a living."

"He lasted four hours on my set before I got security to throw him out on the sidewalk," Ted added with a deep chuckle.

The chatter continued easily as the group reminisced about the people who had come into their lives and those they had lost over the years. Kat listened in fascination to all their stories of what felt like another universe to the one she occupied.

"I don't know about the rest of you, but this old girl needs her beauty sleep, so if you don't mind, I'm going to excuse myself." Martha broke the spell, and everyone agreed her decision was a good one and began tidying up the glasses.

Kat said goodnight and made her way to the *Creaky Cauldron*. When Jordan didn't immediately follow, she felt a flutter of relief. Spending the next fourteen nights with him under her roof was going to take some getting used to, so if he wanted to bunk down on *Dreamcatcher*'s sofa, then she was fine with that.

As it happened, Jordan stumbled into his bedroom at

about two in the morning, whispering loudly to someone on his phone.

She heard him mumbling, 'It's a shitshow,' and 'totally degrading,' and despite being half asleep, her heart ached for Ted and Martha, who clearly only had Jordan's best interests at heart.

Kat stuffed her head underneath her pillow to try to block out the muffled conversation and vowed to pull him up on it in the morning.

It was going to be a long trip.

★ ★ ★

Kat stepped out onto the well deck with a steaming cup of coffee and took a deep breath. The sun hadn't fully risen yet, so the sky had that beautiful yellow-orange wash. Ducks and coots busied themselves along the banks of the canal, and an eager jogger padded down the towpath, giving Kat a cheery wave as he passed by.

The early morning was her favourite time of day. No matter the weather, having her morning coffee outside to greet the day was like a daily meditation ritual that she had to abide by. When her solo guests joined her, they rarely rose from their beds until eight or sometimes later, depending on the activities from the night before, so this had become her precious time and space.

She doubted Jordan would be an early riser, especially after his phone call in the early hours. Looking back at *Dreamcatcher*, she spotted Cole stretching his arms in the air and yawning; his hair stood up in tufts.

"Morning," she called across to him.

He wandered over to her, scratching his chin with one hand and simultaneously rubbing his eyes with the other.

"I wasn't expecting anyone else to be awake yet," he said.

"This is my favourite part of the day. I love the peace and quiet, to be honest, and the coffee always seems to taste better just after the sun comes up." She pointed to the cafetière on the small tray. "Want a cup?"

He hopped onto the deck and flopped onto the seat with an outstretched hand, and Kat chuckled. She made a mental note to remind herself that Cole needed coffee before he was fully functional.

"I don't think I've ever appreciated the outdoors, you know," he said between sips. "I love living in LA, but my apartment is on a busy road with lots of buildings. There's this constant noise of sirens and car horns that you get used to. I think I woke up early because it's so damned quiet."

They laughed, but Kat understood what he meant. It was something a lot of her guests noticed. They weren't used to so much peace and serenity in their lives.

"It can take some getting used to. When I first moved onto the boat, I had an app on my phone that played traffic noise. I'd have it on in the background to help me fall asleep."

He laughed. "Martha's got an app like that, but she's always listening to birdsong or waterfalls. She's going to love this trip."

"One of the things I love about running my business is how the holidays affect people differently. Some of my guests can't abide the quiet for longer than a week, but it gives them a renewed appreciation for their normal noisy life. Other people live in such chaos that a few days on the canal has them selling up and moving to a remote village."

"I'm not sure I'll be selling up, but I intend to take full advantage of the slower pace for a few weeks, that's for sure."

"Is there any coffee left?" Jordan interrupted their conversation as he climbed out of the door, cursing when he knocked his head on the frame.

Without answering, Kat poured him a cup and handed it to him. She didn't receive a thank you, but then she hadn't expected one.

Despite his obvious lack of manners, she couldn't help but appreciate his profile as he lifted the cup to his lips. His tousled hair had that haven't-had-a-good-night's sleep-but-still-look-hot air about it, and his T-shirt hitched slightly as he raised his arm, giving her a peek at the hard wall of muscle hiding underneath.

"Is this Mexican roast?"

His question surprised her, and she quickly raised her eyes from his abs to his face, hoping her cheeks weren't burning with the embarrassment of being caught checking him out.

"Yes, Martha mentioned it was your favourite, so I made sure to stock it for the trip."

"That's a nice touch," he said. His gaze lingered on her for a fraction longer than necessary. "Thank you."

She opened her mouth to say something witty or interesting, but the moment passed as Jordan turned to

Cole. "What's the shooting schedule for today?"

"We plan to capture the *Creaky Cauldron* leaving the marina from a couple of angles," Cole replied. "We'll get a few shots of the front of the narrowboat, the scenery, and you enjoying the views, drinking coffee, and being whimsical in your cable-knit sweater."

Jordan laughed and his entire face changed as the frown he always seemed to wear fell away. He had adorable tiny creases around his eyes that proved he had laughed at least once in his life.

"I'm not sure I'm a whimsical kind of guy," he said, still chuckling. "Maybe we could go with a Captain Jack Sparrow angle. I think I'd make a good pirate."

"We could make that work," Cole said. "Kat, have you got any parrots or eye patches hidden away in this boat of yours?"

Kat giggled at the thought. "I'll see if I can make a ship's wheel to use instead of the tiller, and then you can play pirate when you have a go at steering."

His smile melted away. "I'm not here to drive boats."

Cole looked at the floor as Kat's mouth hung open in disbelief. She gripped her mug a little tighter than necessary and slopped some coffee over the rim.

Their easy conversation ended in a split second as Jordan flipped from the pleasant person enjoying his Mexican roast to the asshole she believed him to be.

What she wanted to do was shout, *That's exactly what you're here to do, you utter wanker*, but she held her breath and counted to ten in her head instead.

As if sensing Kat's building anger, Cole jumped up from

the seat, handed her his empty cup, and hopped back onto the towpath. "I'll go round up the troops," he said, smiling supportively at Kat. "Let's get this adventure started."

Adventure. Why did people keep using that word? This wasn't an adventure; it was a living nightmare. When Stephanie was well enough, Kat was going to kill her for suggesting that this was a good idea. Right now, she was tempted to side with Paul and slink back into her small life where nobody but a select few knew about her and Floating Solo.

★ ★ ★

Martha took the lead as skipper of *Dreamcatcher* when they set off from Mapleton Marina. Roger and Tom had walked over the fields to wave them off, and Kat watched their slow retreat over her shoulder. What would life be like when she saw her friends again? Would she be a shell of her former self, broken by this strange foreign invasion, or would this entire experience build her resilience?

Watching Cole and Ted work was amazing. They bounced off one another, shouting instructions and feedback between the boat and the towpath where Cole was filming their departure.

Kat was at the tiller of the *Creaky Cauldron*, following *Dreamcatcher* at a safe distance. She could see Martha's dark curls and bright red jumper up ahead. Roger had delivered a pair of walkie-talkies to them that morning so the boats could communicate easily without having to rely on their mobile phones, and Kat couldn't resist trying them out.

"This is Cauldron one calling Catcher one. Are you receiving?"

The radio crackled, and Martha's laughter boomed out of the little black box.

"I'm receiving you loud and clear, Cauldron one. The water is clear, and the weather is fine."

Kat chuckled. "Good to hear it. How are you getting on?"

She could see *Dreamcatcher* weaving a little down the canal as Martha got the hang of steering, but so far, she had avoided crashing into the bank.

"Remind me to tape an L and an R to this stick when we stop for lunch."

"Ten-four to that, you're doing great. Take it slow and radio back if you need me."

"Ten-four, over and out."

Kat had total faith in Martha's ability to manage the narrowboat. Ted's plan was to cruise until lunch and then stop so that Kat could take the *Creaky Cauldron* in front and lead the way. They had pinpointed the perfect mooring spot, so all that they needed to do now was relax and enjoy the stunning views.

She knew that Martha wouldn't be able to focus on the passing scenery until she felt more confident with the boat, but Kat felt momentarily sad that everyone else was missing the green fields and hedgerows bursting to life. The Warwickshire countryside was a thing of beauty, and hidden amongst the trees and cottages was an abundance of historical buildings and stories that would keep Ted in business for decades to come.

Cole was jogging alongside the boat with his camera on a gimbal that kept the shots steady even if he was jostling. If nothing else, Kat was learning a lot about what was involved in filming. She had warned the team that the first lock wasn't far along the canal, when it would be safe for Cole to jump back on board. Ted wanted to capture Jordan at the lock, but so far, their star player hadn't left his room.

As if he sensed her animosity, Jordan appeared at the door.

"Did you know I had to walk through your bedroom to get out here?"

Kat didn't acknowledge him. She kept her gaze steady on the horizon and the back of Martha's head as she navigated the boat ahead.

"Yes, I'm well aware of the layout of my boat," she said, trying not to let her words sound as sarcastic as she wanted to be.

"And anyway, who needs that many scatter cushions?"

She blinked in surprise at the mildest hint of humour in his words, breaking her concentration, and glanced down at him as he crawled out of the door. Cole hadn't been joking about the cable-knit jumper, but Kat couldn't deny that Jordan carried it off well. He had chosen cream, which stood out against his lightly tanned skin and made his dark eyes mysterious and almost inviting. His light blue jeans hugged his muscular thighs, and Kat quickly averted her gaze.

He was a pig and didn't deserve any attention. However, Stephanie would be mad at her if she didn't take full advantage of checking him out in such close quarters –

obviously, for research purposes only.

Hugging the back wall of the boat, he stepped to the right of the tiller, which meant he wasn't obstructing her view. It was only in this small space that she realised how tall and muscular he was. Narrowboats, she decided at that moment, were designed for small people.

"Doesn't this thing go any faster?"

"It's not a speedboat!" she snapped. "Narrowboats travel at four miles per hour. It's the law. If you're creating a breaking wave behind you, then you're going too fast. Besides, life in the slow lane is good for the soul."

His forehead wrinkled like that of a small child who was being reprimanded for touching something they shouldn't. Kat watched his gaze flick between her and the horizon before he replied, "I'll have to take your word for it."

Cole had raced ahead and was set up and rolling as they cruised past. Only then did Kat realise Jordan's appearance at the tiller was staged. As she glanced across at his profile, she started giggling. If anyone had asked her what being whimsical looked like, she would not have been able to answer, and yet here she was, witnessing one of Hollywood's biggest stars giving his best performance. It was hilarious to watch. The slight breeze ruffled his hair, and the way he casually rested his elbow on the roof of the boat as if he did this every day made Kat cringe.

"It's incredible to think we're so close to your motorway system and thriving towns. The silence of the canals is almost hypnotic."

Jordan's words stunned Kat, and it took her a few

moments to compose herself enough to respond.

"It's one of my favourite things about living on the water," she said, keeping her eyes on the horizon. "Once you moor, you're in easy distance of everything you need: shops, pubs, doctor, dentist, but being out here on the water is like a secret paradise."

She sensed Jordan glancing across at her and lifted her eyes to meet his. His expression was one of defensiveness mixed with surprise. Was he preventing himself from enjoying this experience? For the first time since meeting him in the car park, she realised Jordan Harrington was a man of many layers. If it took two weeks for him to peel them away then maybe she might get to know the real man behind the movie-star mask.

She was about to mention the historical places they would also pass on their route when Cole interrupted her.

"Got it," he called from the bank, lifting his thumb into the air as he checked the viewfinder on his camera.

Ted's head popped over the top of *Dreamcatcher*'s roof and mirrored the thumbs up. Without the ability to shout 'cut' and stop and start shooting, Ted and Cole had opted for a selection of snippets and continuous footage that their editing team could piece together once they returned to LA.

Kat's head was spinning. Had Jordan staged a polite conversation with her for the benefit of the camera, or was what he had said genuine? She hadn't been given any scripts, but she wondered if he had.

Within seconds, Jordan was inching back along the wall and disappearing back inside.

"Wow, hard work this acting life," she muttered aloud, still trying to work out what was real and what was make-believe.

"I heard that!" Jordan's disembodied voice carried back to her as she stifled a laugh.

In truth, if scripted conversations were the extent of their collaboration, then Kat decided she might enjoy the trip after all.

Chapter Eight

Kat knew from her extensive travels that tourists and day trippers loved standing by the locks watching the narrowboats navigate the watery staircases.

Managing the locks, however, took brute strength and plenty of patience. She wasn't sure how Jordan would react when faced with the gates and paddles, as she was pretty sure he had never done a day of manual labour in his life.

"The general idea is for us to enter an empty lock, fill it up, and then cruise out the other side," she told the crew when they stopped before the first set of locks. "Before we ascend the locks, one of you will run ahead and check if the lock is empty. If it is, you can push against the balance beams to open the gates, I'll steer the boat inside, and then we close the gates behind us."

Beth began wringing her hands as she looked towards the first lock. "I'm not sure I can do this."

"It gets easier the more practice you have, I promise." She gave her arm a reassuring squeeze. "I can do them on my own now, although it takes a lot longer."

"We're all here to help," Cole added, shooting Beth a supportive smile.

Jordan finally surfaced to find out why they weren't moving and strolled along the towpath until he reached the lock gates. Kat encouraged everyone to follow so she could give them all some hands-on training with the windlass.

The confusion and horror etched on each of their faces was priceless, and Kat kicked herself for not capturing that on camera.

Any outsider might think she had asked them to walk the plank. "There's nothing to worry about." Kat laughed, trying to instil some fun into the proceedings.

"Jordan, I want you to take this windlass and slot it onto the paddle mechanism." She handed him the L-shaped handle and showed him where it fitted into the spindle. His hand brushed against hers as she demonstrated, and she resisted the urge to flinch away from him. Instead of his usual disinterest, Jordan seemed to be enjoying his moment in the spotlight. He hadn't even checked to see if Cole was filming.

"Keep a firm grip on the windlass. If it slips out of your hand, it could fly off and injure you."

She watched him set everything up and nodded.

"Perfect. Beth, I need you to cross over to the other side and do the same on that side. When the boat is inside the lock, and the gates are shut behind us, I'll get you both to start winding to let the water in and fill up the lock."

Jordan nodded, his hair flopping into his eyes as he braced himself over the paddle.

"Don't start winding until the boat is inside and the other gates are shut, okay?"

"I'm not stupid," he said, with a slight glint in his eye and what looked like the faintest quiver of a smile. "And I'm not afraid of hard work."

Kat walked away before she embarrassed herself by

saying something she would regret, but she felt a bit lighter that he had been amenable rather than the drama queen she had expected.

Cole and Ted busied themselves setting up the cameras as Kat jumped aboard the *Creaky Cauldron* and steered it inside the lock. She kept the boat in the middle to avoid it catching on anything when the water started rising. Cole and Beth closed the gates behind her before Beth rushed off to the front gate in readiness.

"Okay, guys, if you can both start winding, SLOWLY! And whatever you do, don't let go of the handle," she called up to them, emphasising the slow action to them both.

Jordan wound the paddle, and Kat tried not to focus on the muscles protruding through the cable knit. He seemed to have a knack for it. Beth had also found her rhythm and grinned at Kat as the boat began to rise.

The water began filling the lock and the *Creaky Cauldron* rose an inch at a time. It gave Kat time to grab her phone from her pocket and video Jordan and Beth working on the lock, Cole and Ted filming the pair of them, and Martha sunning herself on a bench.

Once the water was level, Kat called out the next set of instructions.

"Right, I need you both to get your weight behind those gates and open them up so I can cruise out of here."

Beth braced her feet against the tiny brick steps on the floor and pushed as hard as she could. The gate shifted, and she squealed with delight.

"It's just a gate, Beth," Jordan called across to her as he effortlessly pushed his gate open.

"You're doing great, Beth," Kat called out a bit louder in the hope it drowned out Jordan's negativity. "Keep pushing, and then, when I'm out, I need you to close it back up again so we can repeat all of that for *Dreamcatcher*."

"That's my cue," Martha called, uncurling herself from the sunny bench and wandering back to the other boat to get it ready.

Kat kept a close eye on Martha as she navigated the lock, but there had been no need to worry. Both boats cleared the gates and began cruising once again. As Kat settled against the back rail and nudged the tiller, Jordan reappeared at the door.

"I saw you filming us doing the locks earlier," he said, turning his body away from her so he was looking along the length of the boat. "I'm pretty sure Martha would have written into your contract that you weren't allowed to do that. We all want to avoid you selling the footage to the first magazine that gets in touch."

Her grip tightened on the tiller as she listened to the words pour out of his mouth.

"For your information, Beth asked me to capture you all doing the lock and then send her the footage, which I've done *and* deleted off my phone."

She pulled her mobile out of her back pocket and opened the photos app, shoving the screen in his face. "See. The last photo I have on my phone is of my herb pots. Do you want to check my sent messages too?"

He held out his hands. "Okay, okay, I'm sorry. It's just…"

"I'm being paid well to take you on this trip," she interrupted him. "I don't need to sell any story."

"I'm sorry." His voice lowered as he glanced across at her. In that moment he looked lost, and her heart did a strange flip, like she had just put the boat into reverse. "I'm so used to people taking advantage that it puts me on edge."

"I would never do that, Jordan." She didn't know what else to say to him. Seeing his vulnerability for the first time threw her off guard. "All I want is for you all to enjoy the trip and for Ted to get the footage he needs to make your project a success."

His phone rang, breaking the spell, and that dark cloud he always seemed to carry around with him returned.

"I've got to take this," he mumbled before disappearing back inside the boat.

★ ★ ★

Day one on the canal had been a great success despite Jordan's false accusations. The crew had worked together beautifully and managed the locks with growing confidence. They went through a few locks before it was time to moor, and they were blown away by Yarningale aqueduct. Ted and Cole took their time capturing footage of both boats cruising through the narrow bridge that took them over the road, and Beth squealed as she looked down to see cars below her.

"This is crazy," she shrieked, to everyone else's amusement.

Even Jordan came out on deck to witness the aqueduct and seemed suitably impressed.

When Kat saw Beth rubbing the sores on her palms

a little later, she didn't have the heart to tell her that they had another one hundred and twenty-nine locks to go. She decided to save that piece of information for later, perhaps after a couple of glasses of wine.

Apart from his brief appearance at Yarningale, Jordan had been hiding away in his bunk ever since receiving the phone call earlier, but she was pleased that he had taken part throughout the day and not staged his participation in some random movie montage. He had been brilliant with the locks and even stopped to take a few selfies with gobsmacked passers-by.

Despite the day's success, Kat still needed a drink. She had been craving a large glass of red wine since lunchtime and wondered if she could persuade the rest of the crew to enjoy an evening at the gorgeous canal-side pub they had moored next to in Lowsonford.

"Anyone fancy some dinner and a few drinks at the pub?" she called out as she stuck her head inside *Dreamcatcher*.

Within seconds, Beth and Cole appeared, grabbing their shoes and jackets as they jostled each other out of the way.

"Lead the way, Captain," Cole said, giving her a mock salute.

The three of them chatted easily as they walked the short distance down the towpath until they reached the pub. There was plenty of outdoor seating in the grassed beer garden that led down to the canal, and a sea of colourful umbrellas offering shade from the spring sunshine or protection from any spring showers.

In the distance, over the gravel car park, stood the white two-storey building with a terracotta tiled roof. Warm lamplight and relaxed diners filled its tiny windows.

"This is adorable," Beth said, grabbing her phone to film their arrival. "I love your quaint British pubs."

"The beauty of running my Floating Solo business is the ability to visit places like this as often as I can. The pies are amazing too, so it's one of my favourites."

It wasn't long before they ordered and their food arrived. The three of them tucked into homemade dinners washed down with beer and wine. Cole opted for the steak and kidney pie with a pile of chips and a healthy portion of vegetables, while Kat and Beth chose the chicken and mushroom pie and mashed potato. A live band played off to the right with feel-good tunes that had everyone in the pub garden laughing, foot tapping, and singing along.

A patch of grass served as the perfect makeshift dancefloor, and Beth took great delight in dragging Kat up to dance. They whirled and shimmied and laughed until they were breathless. Cole had apprehended Beth's phone and filmed the girls as they lost themselves in the moment and the music. Their exuberance prompted more onlookers to jump to their feet and join the fun.

The staff watched, amused, as the small patch of grass filled with dancing patrons. To anyone passing by, it would have looked like it was New Year's Eve all over again. A tall man with long hair and a bushy beard spun Kat in a wide circle before leading her like he was Anton Du Beke around the crowds to the tune of "Mustang Sally". She laughed until her sides hurt and her cheeks ached.

The opening notes to The Rembrandts' "I'll be There For You" started up, and the crowd erupted in cheers. Some of the diners had moved outside to get in on the action, bringing their half-eaten plates of food along with them.

As one, the crowd clapped and sang along with the verses, drowning out the band, who were in full flow and loving the interaction.

Kat flopped back onto the bench and drained the remnants of her wine before turning to start on the next glass that sat waiting for her.

"You having fun?" Cole asked, laughing at her as Kat mopped her forehead with the cuff of her shirt.

"If I'm honest, I can't remember the last time I had this much fun. It's nights like this that make me wonder what the hell I've been doing with my life."

Cole laughed harder and slapped his hand on her shoulder. "This is what happens when you let the Americans invade your quiet countryside."

The bearded man had moved on to Beth and was whirling her around the grass.

Kat nudged Cole to make sure he was capturing a few photos on the phone. "Is she always this energetic?" She nodded in Beth's direction.

"She's a force of nature, isn't she?"

Kat didn't miss the change in Cole's voice. She glanced up at him, seeing the warmth in his eyes and the small smile as he watched Beth enjoying herself. It was the same way Tom looked at Stephanie. Something she had never experienced for herself.

"You two would make a great couple," she said, testing the waters to see if his look at Beth could be the beginning of a budding relationship.

"No, I'm not her type," he said with a chuckle. "She doesn't want to fall for an old man who'd pull her street cred down."

"Old man! You're twenty-seven for Christ's sake. If you've given up on love at your age, then there's no hope for me."

"Have you given up on love then?"

Kat wasn't sure if she should be offended that Cole's instant response wasn't *oh, but you're still so young*, instead of going straight in for the dirt. She chose to let her thirty-two-year-old ego rise above it.

"I've had one fiancé ditch me just before our wedding, and my current boyfriend of three years needed a break from me, and I'm not sure if he'll be coming back anytime soon."

"It's a low blow on both counts. I'm sorry, Kat," he said, bumping her shoulder with his own and doing the half smile, half shrug she was becoming far too used to. "You should talk to Jordan, though; he's got so many war stories to share about failed relationships and making bad choices that it'll make you feel so much better about yours."

The thought of having such an intimate conversation with Jordan Harrington horrified her, but his relationship dramas had certainly piqued her interest. She wondered if the long line of glamorous women went beyond what she had read online.

Brushing aside any thought of Jordan's love life and

her own disastrous track record, Kat turned her attention back to Cole and Beth.

"I think you'd be surprised about Beth. She looks at you in the same bashful way you do with her."

"Bashful. I've never been called that before." Cole chuckled. "I don't know. She's beautiful; definitely a ten, but I'm only about a seven."

If Kat didn't think it would upset him, she would have screamed with laughter at his words; instead, she opted for a blatantly obvious observation.

"Have you looked in a mirror recently? *You* are a ten. Beth is a ten. Hell, even Ted and Martha, the silver foxes, are sultry senior tens. When you lot got out of the cars back at the marina, I had to pinch myself to check I wasn't dreaming."

Cole roared with laughter at that. "You're too funny, Kat."

"I'm not joking. You guys should be the stars in this docuseries, not me."

Beth bounded up to the table, interrupting them, and downed half a pint of lager. Her face glowed with a light sheen of sweat, and her mascara had smudged slightly under her eyes, but instead of looking like a drunken mess, she appeared to have invented a new smoky eye trend.

"This place is the best!" she squealed. "Come dance with me." She grabbed Cole's hand, and Kat grinned as Beth dragged him towards the band.

Watching the pair of them jumping around, singing loudly and laughing warmed Kat's heart. Maybe having them all in her life, even for a short time, would be cathartic for her. She was so used to being the one who inspired her guests that she had forgotten how it felt to be the one being inspired.

The bearded man reappeared at her side and gently tugged her off the bench and back on the dancefloor. Cole wiggled his eyebrows at her as they whirled past, laughing.

As the night came to a close, the band belted out their final song to enthusiastic cheers and congratulations. The pub landlord began flicking off the lights, and the merry patrons returned to their homes.

Cole and Beth staggered down the towpath, holding one another up, as Kat followed a few steps behind. She giggled as they stumbled and nearly ended up in a hedgerow.

"Don't step too far to the right or you'll end up in the bloody canal," she said, louder than was necessary.

"Ssh, you'll wake everyone up," Beth said, pressing her finger to her lips.

As if on cue, Jordan stepped off *Dreamcatcher*, his face a mask of hostility. "I suggest you get to bed." He moved aside so Cole and Beth could climb aboard and shot a disdainful look in Kat's direction.

"See you in the morning, Kat. Thanks for a brilliant night." Beth blew Kat a kiss before disappearing inside, closely followed by Cole.

"Do you need me to carry you to bed, Miss Sinclair?"

Kat huffed loudly and staggered past him, trying with every muscle in her body to look like she hadn't had far too much to drink. The last thing she wanted was to misstep and fall overboard with Jordan Harrington watching. She was also glad of the cool night air that tempered the heat creeping up her face at the thought of Jordan Harrington carrying her to bed.

"I'm perfectly capable of putting myself to bed, thank you. I don't need some sculpted Adonis to save me."

Jordan pressed his lips together and reached out to steady Kat as she wobbled to the left.

"Perhaps in future, you could avoid getting my staff wasted when they're supposed to be on assignment."

Although Kat was sure there was a genuine reprimand in his words, she didn't miss the hitch in his voice.

She stopped suddenly on the towpath a few paces from the *Creaky Cauldron* and turned slowly to look up at Jordan. In the pale moonlight his chiselled features appeared to shimmer with a pearlescent glow, giving him an angelic aura.

"You are a stuck-up idiot!" she said, jabbing her finger into the hard wall of muscle that was his chest. "You're handsome, yes, but you're wound so tight you would hurt yourself if you ever smiled."

Jordan's eyes flashed with surprise as he looked down at her finger wedged against his chest.

"Maybe if you turned your bloody phone off once in a while, you might actually start enjoying yourself."

With that, she carefully climbed onto the well deck and unceremoniously bounced along every surface until she made it to her bedroom, slamming the door behind her. She didn't bother getting undressed but simply fell into a deep sleep, dreaming about dancing beards and demonic angels.

★ ★ ★

The early morning mist had cleared by the time the crew was dressed and ready to leave. Kat had cooked a big breakfast of bacon, sausage, eggs, baked beans, and buttered toast as a hangover cure, for which Cole and Beth thanked her.

In the deep recesses of Kat's mind, she half remembered a conversation with Jordan the night before where she may or may not have been rude. Until he confirmed this, she chose to believe it had all been a blissful dream. As he hadn't joined them for breakfast, she couldn't gauge if he was mad at her.

Cole wandered off to dismantle the small camera he had fitted at the back of *Dreamcatcher* to capture the *Creaky Cauldron* leaving the marina. Now that they were the lead boat, he wanted to repurpose the camera at the front of Kat's boat to capture their route and the passing scenery.

Her phone vibrated in her pocket, and she pulled it out to see Stephanie's number flash up.

"Hi, how are you?" It had only been just over a day since they left the marina, yet it felt like forever since she had spoken to her friend. "Feeling any better?"

"I'm okay, still a bit grim, but I'm getting there. Have you been on your Instagram account recently?"

"I haven't had a chance, sorry. I know Beth took some photos and a few videos last night when I took her and Cole to the pub, but I'm not sure if she's had time to upload them yet."

"I'm not talking about checking your content. I'm talking about your new followers. Your account has exploded. Tom said that @Beth_Any has been tagging you in on all her behind-the-scenes footage, and it's driving a shitload of people to your page."

"Oh god, is there anything from our night out?"

"Yeah. How dare you go out and have fun without me?" Stephanie laughed. "Kat, it's brilliant. The videos are so much fun, and they're getting loads of positive engagement. It looks like thousands of fans want to see this docuseries when it comes out."

Kat felt like she was in a parallel universe. Here they were in the peace and quiet of the countryside, surrounded by rolling hills and stunning views, and just beyond some invisible veil was a frenzy of fans desperate for a peek into their reality.

"Go check it out. Tom's keeping your page updated and making sure to accept the collaboration requests as they come in from Beth. We've got to keep up with demand."

Stephanie said her goodbyes and hung up, leaving Kat apprehensive about looking at her social media. Her hand shook slightly as she opened her Instagram app. There were fifty-five heart and seventy-nine comment notifications underneath the tiny icon at the top of the screen with one hundred and eighty-two messages.

When Kat clicked on the icon, she saw a flurry of likes on her older posts showing the *Creaky Cauldron*'s interior. The comments were predominantly from young girls who were obviously Jordan's fan demographic. They gushed over the quirky interior and the scenery shots and Kat realised they were probably connecting in the hope of seeing Jordan in one or two of the images.

When she clicked on the messages, they were all linked to the @ mentions Beth had given her on the reels and posts she had created. Tentatively, Kat clicked over to Beth's page and nearly choked at her ninety-seven thousand followers. She began scrolling through the content. Her posts were amazing. They were full of energy, like Beth, with funky emojis and upbeat music. The post from their night out had over seven thousand likes, with comments full of '*love your vibe*' and '*can't wait to see this show*'.

Ted and Martha clearly knew what they were doing by letting Beth run wild with her behind-the-scenes footage. It was building an incredible buzz about the docuseries and, by association, Kat's Floating Solo business.

The reel from the beer garden showed Kat and Beth dancing and laughing, surrounded by a crowd of people all having fun, with the band illuminated in the background. Beth had been kind enough to also tag in the pub and the band so they could reap the benefits of new online connections.

There was a purple hue to the video, cast from the band's lighting, which gave the entire thing a nightclub ambiance. Kat couldn't stop hitting 'watch again' and seeing herself on-screen. It wasn't a vanity thing; it was shock and surprise. She looked happy and carefree, and it suddenly hit her how wrapped up she had been in making Paul happy and trying to build a life that suited him and his world.

'*Stop giving your power away.*' Stephanie's voice floated into her mind as she watched herself whirl around to the music with the bearded stranger.

"Looks like you all had a fun night." Jordan's deep voice interrupted her musings as he watched the video over her shoulder, and she nearly dropped her phone at his sudden appearance. He had a knack for popping up when you least expected it.

"Cole said you had a few admirers vying for a dance," he said, burying his hands deep into his jeans' pockets.

She closed down the app and stuffed her phone back into her jacket.

"Yes, we had a great time, thank you. Maybe you could join us next time. I'll save you a dance." The words were out of her mouth before she could stop herself. What was she thinking?

"Maybe I will, especially if it means I'll avoid a telling-off when you get home." The corner of his mouth twitched slightly in what Kat could only assume was an almost smile as he climbed off the boat and wandered off in Cole's direction.

Holy shit. It wasn't a dream then. She had been rude to him the previous night. She made a mental note to avoid excessive drinking sessions until she learned to control her mouth.

Only after she had finished internally bashing herself did she focus on the potential smile and his comment about her dancing. Jordan had to be the most confusing man on the planet. One minute, he was snapping at everyone and treating her like a teenager sneaking in through the window, and the next, he was smiling, stopping for selfies with fans, and asking about her admirers.

She pulled her phone back out and opened Instagram

again, but this time she brought up Jordan's profile. He had seven million followers and a bio that simply read *Time well spent adds to a life well lived*. His page was full of awards, movie trailers, beautiful women, and an occasional video, but she also noticed that his last post was over seven months ago.

"And I thought I was bad at posting regularly," she mumbled to herself.

The plot thickened. Why was Beth the one doing the 'look at what we are working on' posts and not Jordan? Was there more to this trip than Ted and Martha had let on? If so, Kat intended to find out what.

Chapter Nine

Life on the cut was only part of the experience Kat wanted to share with her guests. It was also important that she included the occasional sightseeing jaunt and cultural encounter.

She had already run her idea past Martha and Ted, who agreed that a day off the boats would be great for the docuseries. With the peace and quiet of canal life momentarily shattered as they crossed over the M40 motorway, Kat was already wondering if Jordan would join them or choose to stay behind on the boat. He had popped his head out of his bunk more often during the course of the day to check on progress and had run back to *Dreamcatcher* for a catch-up with Ted, but on the whole, he was keeping himself to himself.

They had navigated several locks and were approaching The Wharf Tavern, their evening mooring spot. It was the perfect place to stretch their legs, grab a few essentials from the local shops, and enjoy a hearty dinner at the pub.

As they continued along the Avon Ring over the days to come, most evenings would be spent on the boats with homecooked meals, conversation, laughter, and wine, but Kat wanted to include some of the local pubs and restaurants as she knew how important it would be for them to appear in the finished docuseries.

She was happy that they were a couple of days into the trip and nobody had fallen overboard, that everyone was still getting along, and that Stephanie was almost back to her usual healthy self.

"I need my gossip quota," Stephanie said down the phone as Kat stood at the tiller, navigating down a particularly beautiful stretch of canal.

"I can only give you what's happening," Kat said with a soft chuckle. "If they don't do anything gossip-worthy, I can't deliver."

"I know, I know. Beth's posts have been entertaining me, and I love the variety of reels, although I noticed the big Hollywood star hasn't ventured into the galley to cook anything yet."

Kat raised her eyebrows and then realised Stephanie couldn't see her. "Hmm, he seems to be allergic to pots, pans, washing-up liquid, and sewage-holding tanks."

Stephanie laughed. "Oh, please get me a video of him emptying the poo."

"I think it's more likely you'll see a flying pig on one of Beth's reels," Kat said with a snort. "Besides, tonight I'm taking them to The Wharf Tavern, where they have the patio alongside the canal. No cooking for any of us this evening, so watch out for the new footage."

"Wear something sexy and see if you can get a slow dance with Jordan. That'll do wonders for your page likes."

"Are you pimping me out to random Hollywood stars in a bid to boost my profile?"

"Hell yeah!" Stephanie laughed.

It felt like the world was back on its axis.

"Have you heard from Paul?"

The sudden shift in topic threw Kat for a second and she shook her head as if to dislodge the new direction their conversation was heading in.

"Not since we agreed to take a bit of a break. I've been busy dealing with the current drama you signed me up for. Why do you ask?"

"Hmm? Oh, we saw him in town, and he said he was going to call you."

"Well, he's not the most reliable man we know, but I'm sure he'll call when he's ready."

Stephanie signed off with her usual well wishes, but there was something strange in her tone. Although she sounded like she was back to her old self, Kat did worry that Stephanie's recent illness had wiped her out more than she was willing to admit.

There was nothing she could do to help her friend from where she was, but she vowed to check in more often.

Their mooring for the night was up ahead, and pushing thoughts of Stephanie and Paul aside, she radioed back to Martha with instructions. They all worked well together when it came to operating the narrowboats and getting them moored up for the night, and she was excited about taking the crew out for drinks. It felt like she was rewarding them for good behaviour – even Jordan.

The boys were ready first and made their way to the pub, leaving Kat, Beth, and Martha finishing up with hairdryers and make-up.

"Get the drinks in," Kat called after them, and Cole gave her a thumbs up.

She had already dressed in slim jeans and a fitted blouse, but as Jordan had hogged the bathroom, Kat had to go join the girls on *Dreamcatcher* to do her hair and make-up.

Beth jumped at the chance to curl Kat's hair into waves and fix her eyes so they looked mysterious.

"You better get a good photo of this, because I'll never be able to replicate it when you leave me," Kat said, staring at her reflection.

They were only twenty minutes behind the boys, but when they arrived at the pub, Jordan was missing.

"How do you misplace a six-foot man?" Kat asked, glancing around the large outdoor beer garden.

"Oh, we didn't misplace him." Cole grinned, nodding to the far side of the patio. "We filmed him doing the celeb thing at the bar and in the crowds, and now we've left him in good hands."

A group of five young women were draped over Jordan's shoulders, taking selfies and giggling. Kat turned away, unsure why it bothered her so much that he would choose to spend the night with strangers over their little group. Ted and Martha were deep in conversation and seemed oblivious to Jordan's interactions, and Beth had already drained her first glass of wine and was weaving her way to the bar.

"You better keep an eye on her tonight; otherwise Jordan will be telling us off again when we get home," Kat said, pointing after Beth.

Cole grinned up at her and shot off after the pretty

blonde. It was so obvious they liked each other, and she hoped that in the right environment and with a bit of gentle nudging, they would get together. Her own relationships were an utter disaster, but playing cupid for her new friends was a relationship role she could get on board with.

"The menu looks great," Ted said, interrupting her thoughts.

"They're famous for the chicken wings," she replied, glancing back over to see Jordan sitting on a bench with his arms around two of the girls. Their high-pitched laughter made Kat's teeth itch.

After much deliberation, they all ordered and settled themselves in for their meal. Cole and Beth returned with another round of drinks, and they all slid into their usual easy conversations.

"Where are you taking us tomorrow, Kat?" Martha asked as she waved her mobile in the air. "I'm on with the chauffeur company."

"Warwick Castle."

Martha relayed the information, confirmed the numbers – six, which meant Jordan was coming with them – and ended the call.

"I'm looking forward to a day on land."

"Aren't you enjoying life on board?" Kat teased. She knew how it could take people time to find their sea legs.

"Oh, no, I didn't mean that. I love the boats, but my old knees are grateful for firm foundations once in a while."

They all laughed as Martha pulled a face and rubbed at her knees.

"How is your schedule going?" Kat asked Ted, interested in the entire filmmaking process.

"We're getting a lot of great shots, and there's some incredible scenery to capture, but we're going to need to get a few more action frames of you and Jordan in the *Creaky Cauldron*. It's the whole Floating Solo holiday experience I want to capture."

Kat had been afraid of that. She knew the time was coming when she would need to play the host and take a more central role in the filming. In Martha's initial emails, it was laid out that the docuseries had to look like Jordan had booked a solo holiday and was enjoying all the tasks that her usual guests took part in.

Maybe the day she did manage to film him emptying the poo was on the horizon. The thought of him dealing with the holding tanks raised a sly smile. She glanced across to where he had made himself at home with the locals, but Jordan was gone. Some of the girls still remained at the table, but the two blondes he had been hugging were also missing.

If he ended up back at one of their houses, then Kat hoped he set his alarm in the morning; otherwise, she was tempted to leave for their day trip to Warwick Castle without him.

Ted and Martha had returned to *Dreamcatcher* an hour earlier, and it appeared likely that Cole and Beth were settling down for a long night of drinking.

"I can't do another heavy night, guys. I'm not as young as I used to be. I'm going to head back."

"Do you want us to walk you home?" Cole asked.

"No, I'm okay. You stay and have fun." She looked pointedly at Cole as she said it, and he smiled. Hopefully, tonight was the night he told Beth how he felt.

The cool night air was refreshing as Kat strolled down the towpath back to the *Creaky Cauldron*. The sky was full of stars, and there wasn't a soul around. She took a moment to be still and gaze up at the wonder of the universe stretched out above her. Although she was having a lot of fun with the crew, she did crave those calm and quiet moments.

In the distance, she could see *Dreamcatcher* in total darkness, Ted and Martha opting for an early night, but the *Creaky Cauldron* was lit up like a fairground. Every lamp was on, and the curtains were wide open, so the towpath and hedgerows were illuminated in the splash of yellow light. As she drew closer, she could hear the music as it blared out, echoing across the canal and neighbouring countryside. "So much for waterways' etiquette," she muttered to herself.

Staring through the windows of her living room, she felt sick to her stomach. Jordan was stripped down to his dark grey boxers and T-shirt, swigging from a bottle of wine as one of the blonde girls from the bar clung to him, wearing nothing but her underwear.

The other girl, who was also missing her clothes, languished on Kat's sofa, hugging one of her scatter cushions to her ample bosom.

Kat stormed onto the well deck and burst through the door, making the girls yelp in fright.

"What the hell are you doing?" she screamed, staring at Jordan and ignoring the half-naked girls.

"We're playing strip poker," he said with a wink at the girls, who had the good sense to laugh nervously while keeping an eye on Kat. She wondered if she looked as crazy-eyed as she felt.

Kat ignored the fact that no pack of cards was anywhere to be found and flipped the off switch on the radio, plunging the interior of the boat into a sudden and deafening silence. She began scooping up the discarded clothes and shoes.

"Get out of here," she said, her voice hard and her stare cold. She marched back outside and proceeded to throw the girls' clothes onto the towpath.

"Hey, what the hell are you doing?" the blonde, who was still attached to Jordan, yelled after Kat. "That's my dress."

"I suggest you get the hell off my boat and retrieve it then." The bitterness in Kat's voice and the raw anger she felt rising up from her feet startled even her.

"Freak!" the first girl mumbled as she stumbled past Kat and onto the path.

"Jeez, you're a nutter," said the other girl before turning back to Jordan with a pout. "Aren't you going to tell her to mind her own business, Jordy?"

"GET OUT!" Kat screamed.

The girl jumped and rushed outside, almost falling headlong into the hedgerow as she lost her footing. They picked up their clothes and began half walking, half dressing as they scurried away, directing a constant barrage of abuse and obscenities as they retreated.

Kat waited for what felt like forever before closing the door, locking it, and turning to face Jordan.

He stood in the middle of her living room, swaying slightly on his feet, with a deep scowl on his face. "How dare you embarrass me like that?" he slurred. "You had no right to come in here and kick them out."

"I have *every* right, you insensitive, entitled prick!" Kat yelled. "You have zero respect for anyone. Not for me, Ted, Martha, Cole, or Beth. You think the world owes you a fucking living, and you don't give a damn who you trample on to get what you want. Yes, you get to enjoy my hospitality, and yes, I might be the hired help, but this boat isn't some random rental or Airbnb where you can hook up with slutty strangers. This is my *home*!"

Jordan glared at her for a long while, but she held his gaze, her eyes burning with fury. Eventually, he glanced around him as if seeing the interior for the first time.

To his left was the built-in shelving unit with her favourite books, and photos of her and her father beside the personal trinkets she had picked up on her travels. Next to that was her dad's old record collection and photo albums. Over by the kitchen was the gallery of photographs she had collected over the years with a sea of sweet, happy, and grateful guests.

Kat bent over to pick up the cushions from the sofa and began setting everything back in its place. Tears streamed down her face as she moved methodically around the boat.

She grabbed Jordan's jeans last and threw them in his face. "Here you go, Jordy," she mimicked before storming off to her bedroom and slamming the door.

She didn't try to conceal her loud sobs, part of her

hoping each one would be a punch in the gut to Jordan Harrington.

★ ★ ★

No amount of make-up could help Kat go from puffy-eyed and pale-faced to camera ready by the time the crew got up and started a new day.

It had taken every ounce of her strength to climb out of bed after the memory of the previous night's events tumbled to the forefront of her mind.

Would Ted and Martha pack up and head home after everything she had said to Jordan? Yes, he had been in the wrong, but he was also the star of the show and no doubt they all expected a modicum of respect from the host.

Getting from her bedroom to the main living space meant walking past Jordan's bunk, which was only separated from the corridor by a heavy curtain. The fabric, however, was pulled back, revealing an empty bed.

There was no way he would have been up early after the state he had been in the previous night, so Kat was either going to find him passed out on the sofa or he would have taken himself off to *Dreamcatcher*. As she poked her head around the corner of the bathroom and saw the living room and galley were empty, she let out the breath she had been holding onto.

She made the coffee extra strong and chose the largest mug she owned before pouring herself a cup.

The clock on her phone read 05.45, which meant Stephanie would not appreciate a call this early even though the gossip was juicy. Instead, Kat climbed outside, dropped onto the bench seat on the well deck, and sipped her drink.

What had she been thinking? She understood herself well enough to know why she reacted the way she did when he disrespected her home, but why had it bothered her so much that he was with those girls in the first place?

Jordan Harrington was an asshole. She had established that within the first few seconds of meeting him. And yet, over the past couple of days, she had seen the smallest slivers of a decent human being. Granted, they were rare moments, but if he was capable of decency, then maybe he wasn't the awful person she was making him out to be.

Stephanie would have supplied a long list of reasons why caring what Jordan said and did mattered to her. Deep down, all she really wanted was to surround herself with people she could trust.

Her fiancé abandoned her before their wedding; her father abandoned her by dying before his time, and even Paul abandoned her on a personal and professional level. Was it too much to ask that the people in her life stuck around when they said they would and treated her with respect?

"Am I interrupting?" Martha's soft voice made Kat jump.

"No, not at all. I wasn't expecting to see anyone up and about yet." She motioned for Martha to join her and scurried off to get another mug of coffee.

"Thank you," Martha said, gratefully taking the steaming mug.

They sat in silence for a while, watching the hedgerows and canal burst to life with the birds, bees, and voles scurrying about their business. The air was fresh, and the sky was clear, which meant they were in for a beautifully sunny spring day.

"In case you were wondering, Jordan slept on *Dreamcatcher*," Martha said quietly, in between sips of coffee. "He was furious, but I think he was more humiliated than anything."

There was no accusatory tone to her voice, nor did she appear angry, but Kat understood that Martha needed details to fill in the gaps. She was an intelligent woman and knew how to gather the facts before passing judgement. Martha was also Jordan's agent, which meant his welfare was her priority.

Although Kat had no need to apologise, she felt compelled to where Martha was concerned.

"I'm so sorry," she said in a rush. "It was highly unprofessional of me. If you decide to cut the trip short, I fully understand and will reimburse you."

"My dear Kat, what on earth are you apologising for? From what I could gather from Jordan's garbled, drunken ranting, *he* was the one in the wrong, not you."

Kat's shoulders relaxed, and she slumped back on the seat, realising she had been holding her body rigid. "Thank you. I totally lost my temper last night, and I said some terrible things to Jordan."

"I believe you told him he was entitled, insensitive, and disrespectful."

Kat cringed. She really hadn't held back.

"I don't regret saying those things because I believe them in my heart, but I will admit, it was unprofessional. I don't know Jordan well enough to speak to him like that, and I probably should have spoken to you first."

Martha chuckled. "I don't think any person on the planet would stay professional when finding half-naked women in their living room."

Kat smiled. Martha understood, and that mattered more to her than Martha would ever realise.

"Besides, Jordan needed to hear it." Martha stood up as if the action gave her the courage to say whatever she needed to. "We've coddled him for too long. Everything you said to him is true, and it's my fault for trying to protect him instead of being honest."

Kat was shocked by the revelation. After watching the group interact over the past couple of days, she had assumed that everyone ignored Jordan's rudeness because they were used to him being that way. Now it appeared they were all hiding something. What was Martha trying to protect Jordan from?

"You love him like a son," Kat said, trying to reassure Martha that whatever she needed to do was worth doing. "Sometimes, we need to hear the hard truths to move on with our lives."

Yes, she was saying the words for Martha's benefit, but what she was saying also resonated with her.

Her fiancé hadn't been right for her, and his leaving shouldn't have come as a surprise. He had tried to talk to her, tried to tell her that things weren't right, but she had been so invested in building a life that she painted over the cracks. It was a hard truth she had refused to accept.

When her father told her he had cancer, she stuck her head in the sand and couldn't allow herself to believe it was as bad as the doctors were telling her. Another hard truth she hadn't wanted to face.

Paul was the only one who had been open and honest with her, but instead of listening to what he had to say, she had got angry and lashed out – just like Jordan.

The similarities between herself and Jordan hit her full in the chest. They were both battered, bruised, and a little broken.

"I do think of him as a son, and Ted feels the same about him, which is why we keep pushing for him and doing our best, but I don't think our best is good enough. Not without Jordan knowing the truth."

"What is the truth?" Kat needed to know. She suddenly felt a sense of responsibility, as it was her fault this had all come to a head.

"Jordan believes that we're turning down roles on his behalf because he's too big for the parts, but the honest truth is nobody will hire him."

Kat's mouth fell open slightly. She knew Jordan as a big Hollywood star who was the main character in almost all her favourite films. He was always splashed over the glossy magazines, and snippets of him accepting awards filled her For You page on TikTok.

"Are you telling me he's unemployable and he doesn't know?" Kat asked.

"That's exactly what I'm saying. This docuseries is our last attempt at redemption. We want to show him in a different light. The casting directors see a petulant man with no respect, who is insensitive, argumentative, and entitled."

No wonder Kat's harsh words hit home with Martha when she found out about her argument with Jordan.

"Beth's behind-the-scenes footage on her personal Instagram is an attempt to try and show the softer side of Jordan," Martha continued. "We want people to see the real him, or rather, the man he used to be before…"

"Before what?" Kat, perched on the edge of the bench, was fully invested in what Martha was telling her.

"His relationships have been an issue," Martha said carefully. "The women he chooses aren't in it for romance and flowers."

Kat thought back to a recent interview she had watched with Lexi Chivers, Jordan's current girlfriend. The journalist had referred to it as 'explosive' but refused to expand on their observations. Lexi was the lead on a high-grossing Netflix show, and it always seemed like everyone loved her, but Kat remembered her throwaway comment about benefitting from her circle of friends and lovers to build her career.

"Does Lexi know Jordan isn't getting work?"

Martha visibly bristled at the mention of Lexi's name. "That woman is a pariah," she said through gritted teeth. "We have had to do a lot of damage control where she is concerned, but Jordan won't see how toxic she is."

Kat recalled all of Jordan's late-night and early-morning phone calls that had kept her awake. Had he been speaking to Lexi?

"Are they still a couple?" The words stuck in the back of Kat's throat.

"She tells the world they're soulmates, but I would like to think that Jordan is starting to see her for what she is. When we first told him about the docuseries and coming to England, he wanted Lexi to come with us, but Ted put his foot down. Jordan was furious, and Lexi went public with her lies about Ted trying to come between them."

"That's awful. Ted is the sweetest man I've ever met."

"I think Lexi went too far by badmouthing Ted," Martha said. "Jordan agreed to the trip without telling her, and so she did her usual trick of jumping on social media, this time to tell the world she and Jordan were over. It's all a big publicity stunt, of course. She gets thrust into the limelight as a victim, and Jordan gets seen in a bad light – yet again."

"Has he been in touch with Lexi recently?" If Martha was unaware of the phone calls, then perhaps Kat had a duty to tell her.

"He's constantly on the phone with her," Martha said, freeing Kat of any obligation to spill the beans. "We keep trying to engage him in this trip and the filming, but he's never far from his phone and that woman spitting venom into his ear."

"If Jordan and Lexi believe you're the ones turning down work on his behalf, then Lexi will probably be telling him to leave you and Ted, fly back to America, and be the big superstar she still thinks he is."

A dog walker sauntered past and tugged at the lead as his Labrador tried to chase after a duck down the towpath.

Martha sat back down and nursed her coffee mug. Her shoulders slumped forward slightly in an exhausted, almost defeated manner. How long had Martha and Ted been covering for Jordan and trying to keep his dwindling career alive?

"I think it's time that Ted and I told Jordan exactly what's going on," she said softly.

Chapter Ten

Despite Kat understanding more about Jordan being the way he was, she couldn't bring herself to actively engage with him civilly yet. She was still fuming about his antics in her living room, for which he hadn't apologised.

She knew Martha and Ted planned to talk to Jordan, but she didn't know when they were going to drop that bombshell. Maybe Ted would get the bulk of the filming done first so it didn't interrupt their schedule. Or would they tell Jordan the truth and use his reaction as part of the docuseries?

Whatever they decided to do, Kat knew there would be fallout, and she felt like she had to be cautious about what she said and did around him.

Spending the day sightseeing was a blessing in disguise. She and Jordan could avoid each other but not interrupt Ted's filming schedule. There were plenty of places to hide in the castle and grounds.

"They've got a falconry exhibition," Beth squealed. "I love birds."

Kat chuckled at Beth's enthusiasm as they passed under the portcullis, clutching their VIP tickets.

"I've seen that show a few times, and it's definitely

worth it. They have about fifty or sixty different birds of prey flying over your head."

"Sounds great. Ted, Ted, can we do the Falconer's Quest?"

Beth tugged on Ted's arm like an impatient child until he rolled his eyes and gave in to her demands.

"Let me check with the staff about what we can and can't include if we do any filming." He motioned to one of the staff, who came scurrying over to help.

"I've got maps," Cole said, brandishing the colourful leaflets that pinpointed all of the attractions.

"Where do you recommend we start?"

Kat turned to answer the question directed at her and was surprised to see it was Jordan who had asked it. His shoulders were hunched over slightly, and he wore a dark baseball cap pulled down low.

After looking at the state of her blotchy face in the mirror before they left the boats, Kat had opted for a cap of her own teamed with the biggest sunglasses she could find.

She and Jordon looked a right sorry pair.

"If anyone wants to start with a coffee, I'd recommend the Conservatory Tea House by the Peacock Garden," she said.

Jordan and Martha nodded simultaneously at her suggestion.

"Ooh, can we do the maze?" Beth was bouncing up and down, which made the rest of the group chuckle. She was worse than a toddler.

"Cole, why don't you take Beth to the maze, we'll head to the tea house, and we can meet up at the riverside for the falconry show?"

Kat didn't miss the sparkle in Cole's eyes at the thought of spending time alone with Beth, but his duty to Ted clearly prevented him from rushing off into the high hedges.

As if sensing his dilemma, Ted smiled and said, "We'll get no filming done if Beth doesn't have some fun first. Go, enjoy yourselves. We can scope out the entire site and return to any places that would make good backdrops."

Beth and Cole didn't wait for Ted to finish his sentence before sprinting off in the direction of the maze.

"They do know it's for kids, don't they?" Jordan said with a touch of humour in his voice.

"You're never too old for Horrible Histories," Kat said with a chuckle.

Jordan smiled down at her, and she felt suddenly exposed despite the oversized sunglasses.

"The tea house is this way," she mumbled, walking in the direction of the conservatory and hoping the others would follow.

Kat had been prepared for a moody, monosyllabic Jordan after what she had screamed at him the previous night, but she wasn't equipped for an about-turn in his entire personality. Had Martha already spoken to him? No, she wouldn't have had time between their early morning chat and the cars arriving to transport them to Warwick.

As the beautiful stone building with its high arched windows rose up in front of them, she turned to find Martha and Ted walking in the opposite direction and Jordan kicking a stone along the path behind her.

"Where are they going?" Her voice hitched in panic.

"Martha wanted to get a photo," he said, pointing towards the entrance of the main castle. "They'll join us inside."

Kat's pulse quickened at the thought of being alone with Jordan, but not in an excitable way. She wasn't sure how she would handle any aggression on his part if he wanted to vent about her behaviour towards him.

The conservatory wasn't busy yet, so they chose one of the window seats where they could look out over the gardens and fountains. Jordan ordered two cappuccinos and settled into the seat beside her. They sat in silence for a while, watching the excited tourists milling about on the patio and listening to the undeniable call of the peacocks.

"I'm sorry for what happened last night," Jordan said finally, breaking the silence. "I was out of line in a million ways."

He rubbed his palms along the tops of his legs, and Kat realised with a jolt that he was nervous.

"For what it's worth, I shouldn't have called you all those horrible names," she replied. "Or been rude to your friends."

She choked out the last bit, but just in case his brief union with the two blondes resulted in lifelong friendships for him, she didn't want that hanging over her.

"I don't think I'll be seeing those women again," he said with a weak smile. "Although I'm pretty sure if you hadn't come back when you did, Martha would be mopping up another scandal sold to the media."

It hadn't dawned on Kat that those girls might have

taken advantage of the situation in such a way, but it made her feel a tiny bit better about throwing them out.

"Why do you do it?" she asked before she could stop herself.

He glanced at her but stayed silent, and Kat worried she had overstepped. Just as she was about to change the subject he started speaking.

"Have you ever felt so disconnected that all you crave is an honest conversation and to surround yourself with people you can trust? But when you try and connect, all you get back are lies and empty promises?"

Kat's breath caught at his words. Hadn't she had the exact thought about her own life only a matter of hours ago? How was it possible that she and Jordan were so alike?

"If the people you meet in bars go out of their way to hurt you, why hook up with them in the first place? No disconnection is worth that."

Jordan lifted his head and stared out of the window. The early morning sunshine hit the side of his face like a bright aura and highlighted the curve of his jaw. Finally he spoke.

"About six or seven months ago I got involved with a woman who, on the surface, was sweet, funny, and beautiful. Me and Lexi were on one of our breaks at the time. I dated Joanna for a while, and she even moved some of her stuff into my apartment." He paused to add a sachet of sugar to his drink. "I thought it was the real thing, but it turned out Lexi had slept with Joanna's husband, and she was only out for revenge."

He stirred his coffee a little more vigorously than necessary and slopped some over the side into the saucer.

"The husband was still on the scene and came at me with a baseball bat outside my apartment complex. I defended myself a little too well, and he ended up with a broken nose. Joanna went to the papers."

Six or seven months ago? That explained why Jordan hadn't posted on his Instagram for a while.

As if reading her mind, he added, "I might have added a few drunken rants once or twice on my social media accounts, and so Martha had to ban me from using my own sites. She changed the passwords so I couldn't access my pages and deleted all the posts I'd put out." He smiled, but it didn't reach his eyes. "I guess it's in my nature to act like an idiot."

Kat took off her sunglasses and laid them on the table next to her coffee cup. All she wanted to do was reach out and squeeze his hand, but she couldn't risk him getting angry at her or him thinking it was a pity party.

He looked across at her and flinched as he took in her bloodshot eyes and blotchy face.

"I really am sorry for not respecting your home," he said.

"You're forgiven," she whispered. There was so much more she wanted to say to him, but the moment passed as Martha and Ted arrived.

Kat chatted along with Martha as Ted ordered more drinks. She told them all about the ghost stories associated with the castle and pointed out her recommendations for filming locations, but somewhere in the back of her mind, she was still processing what Jordan had told her.

How would he react when Martha finally told him

the truth? There were more lies for him to digest, more empty promises. It was hard for Kat to stay angry at him, knowing how broken and alone he was. Who did he have in his life besides the small crew he travelled with? She was suddenly even more appreciative of Stephanie and Tom. Having friends she could trust meant she would never end up like Jordan Harrington.

Although they were only at the start of their Floating Solo trip, the day out at Warwick Castle was a big hit. Beth squealed throughout the Falconry Quest, shooting some amazing behind-the-scenes videos of her and Martha as the bald eagle soared just above their heads. Even Ted yelped a couple of times as the incredible birds of prey skimmed the top of the seated crowds.

Kat sat in the late spring sunshine, watching Cole working the camera and Ted directing Jordan as he sauntered up and down the hundreds of stone steps set into the towers and ramparts. The group had begun to attract a small following of fans, which meant the filming had more of a stop-start rhythm than continuous footage.

Beth captured plenty of fan engagement with Jordan as he chatted easily with anyone who stopped to talk to him. Ted would keep rolling when the crowds dispersed, and Martha would hover at his shoulder, sharing her own thoughts and directions.

For a moment, Kat felt like she was living in a TV show. One second, she was watching them filming from across the courtyard and the next, she was included in the montage. At one point, Ted asked her to join

Jordan as he descended the tight staircase from the Time Tower, where the steps were a little steeper and the space narrower.

They bumped shoulders on nearly every step until Jordan paused halfway down, sweeping his arm out and shouting, "M'lady" so Kat could go first. She giggled and skipped down the rest of the steps, much to Ted's delight.

"Great shot!" he said before pointing at the ice-cream truck for his next scene.

When they were on the boats, the filming didn't feel so structured. Perhaps it was because most of the cameras were practically hidden or that Cole was on the towpath or that *Dreamcatcher* was further away. If this experience taught Kat anything, it would be never to fear creating video reels for her social media ever again.

They all stretched out on the grass, tucking into ice-cream cones topped with strawberry whirls and chocolate flakes. Jordan sat next to Kat with his arm brushing up against her. She tried to focus on the trickle of vanilla ice cream as it trailed a path down the cone. Instead, it was the closeness of his body that caught her attention until Beth stole the chocolate flake from Cole, which began a cat-and-mouse chase through the courtyard.

As Kat laughed at the scene, Jordan bumped her shoulder and brandished his mint choc chip. "Want to try some of mine?"

Stunned by the casual friendliness of his action, she leaned forward only to end up with the ice cream daubed on the end of her nose.

Jordan's face lit up as he laughed.

"Oh, this is war," Kat said, jumping to her feet and brandishing her vanilla ice cream like a sword.

At that moment Jordan's mobile rang and Kat watched the familiar dark cloud pass over his face as he looked at the caller ID. He stood up and walked across the courtyard as he accepted the call.

Martha and Ted exchanged a look but said nothing.

Behind the relative privacy of her sunglasses, Kat couldn't tear her eyes away from Jordan, who was now pacing outside the Great Hall. His brow furrowed as he listened to whoever was on the other end, although Kat guessed at it being Lexi Chivers. Jordan's entire posture had changed in a matter of moments. The laid-back energy of the entire day fell away and seemed to puddle at his feet, replaced by tension and sharp edges.

Although she couldn't hear his conversation, she knew it wasn't a loving exchange between a happy couple. Even she and Paul had managed to hold civil conversations with one another on a bad day.

Jordan pushed the button on his phone and shoved it back into his jeans' pocket before spinning back in their direction.

"And that's our cue to get the hell out of here," Cole mumbled.

Almost as one, the crew stood up and started collecting their things and packing away the camera and gimbal. Half-eaten ice creams were discarded into the bins. Nobody said anything. Nobody approached Jordan to find out how he was, and no one asked who had called.

In a daze, Kat followed them all back to the Range

Rovers and watched the streets and houses rush by as they headed back to where they had moored the boats.

Jordan sat in the back of the car with her as Martha took the front passenger seat. He didn't speak. Martha chatted to the driver and occasionally threw a question back to Kat, but Jordan remained silent, staring out of the window. His energy was flat, and his shoulders were hunched. The baseball cap he had taken off during the day was back in place and pulled down low once again.

As soon as they arrived at the boats, he scurried off to his bunk.

"It's best if you leave him alone," Martha said as they stood on the towpath alongside the *Creaky Cauldron*. "He'll process it all in his own time and come back to us when he's ready."

Kat nodded her understanding, but she had to fight every instinct she had to find Jordan and give him the opportunity to talk through whatever was on his mind. Maybe she had been hanging around with Stephanie for too long, but leaving people to wallow in their own misery only created a victim mentality. Was this part of the problem? Perhaps Martha and Ted should be more proactive with Jordan. Whatever was going on, she suddenly felt uncomfortable staying on the boat knowing Jordan was inside.

As she perched on the bench seats outside and watched the ducks waddle along the canal, a wave of longing washed over her for Paul and the semblance of a normal relationship. Yes, they were taking a break, but did she honestly believe it would be forever? No. What they had was worth fighting for, and when he did eventually get back in touch she knew what she had to do.

★ ★ ★

After a lovely day at Warwick Castle, the crew did their own thing at night. Nobody suggested a group meal or a trip to the pub, and Jordan's absence meant Kat ended up eating a bowl of soup on her own at the breakfast bar.

She heard whispers again late at night as the phone calls continued, but she was so tired from their excursion that she rolled over and pulled the quilt over her head.

Her early morning coffee on the deck always brightened her day, and it wasn't long before the two boats were cruising the cut again.

Ted had left instructions that Jordan would be needed when they moored up at lunchtime, but so far, the star had remained in his bunk.

The next few days were all about the Floating Solo experience, which Kat felt fully qualified to supply. However, with the recent tension between her and Jordan and his sporadic behaviour, it proved harder than usual.

"Right, can I get Jordan and Kat in the galley making lunch?" Ted called from the towpath, interrupting Kat's moment of quiet contemplation. They had moored up for a break and to capture more stills and were enjoying half an hour sitting in the spring sunshine.

Knowing full well the inner turmoil Ted and Martha were going through, Kat decided it was time to rise above it and get on with the show.

She waited in the galley for Jordan to join them and pottered around, cleaning the sink and wiping down the worksurface. If there was one thing she didn't want to see in the docuseries, it was an untidy kitchen.

"What's on the menu?" Jordan asked as he joined Kat in the small galley. His large frame filled the space, making movement difficult without brushing up against each other.

"Ted wants us to make a chicken Caesar salad," she said before adding, "I understand it's your favourite."

Jordan's expression shifted briefly as if he had been expecting more tension instead of a simple conversation.

"It is. I'm a sucker for a crouton."

Kat giggled without meaning to, and Jordan smiled in response.

Cole and Ted bustled around them, moving cameras and repositioning the crockery so they were in the front of the shot.

"I want you to act naturally," Ted said. "Kat, you're making lunch and showing your latest guest where the utensils are and how easy it is to prepare lunch in a narrowboat."

Kat was pretty sure she had never taught a guest how to make lunch before. They usually perched on the high stools and watched her. As Jordan's arm brushed against her for the fifth time, she decided to mention this small fact to the director.

"Ted, when my guests are on board, they usually sit over there." She pointed at the other side of the counter towards the stools. "I prepare the food, and they relax."

Jordan took a step back as if her comment was a personal insult.

"I'm happy to do it your way, but it might look more natural if it was more laid-back."

After a short deliberation and a couple of minor alterations to the cameras, Ted agreed to her set-up. Jordan perched on the high stool, his elbows leaning on the counter and his chin resting on his folded hands, while she readied herself to make the salad.

"Camera rolling."

"How long have you lived on board the *Creaky Cauldron*?" Jordan asked as she washed the mixed lettuce leaves. She felt uncomfortable, as if washing lettuce was something she had never done before. Knowing the cameras were rolling made a perfectly normal activity feel weird.

"Four years," she said eventually.

"What made you decide to live on the water?"

Once the lettuce was ready, she divided it between the two bowls. Then she moved to the chopping board and began slicing the pre-cooked chicken breasts before answering.

"After my dad died, I used to go down to the marina to feel close to him. When I was younger, he would take me to see the boats every weekend, and we got to know a lot of the people who lived on the water. It seemed like the most logical place to be after he'd gone."

There was a long silence and Kat glanced up to see Jordan watching her. She was about to ask him a question when he jumped in first.

"Tell me about your father."

His request floored her. Apart from Roger, Paul, Stephanie and Tom, nobody else in her world talked to her about her dad. People rarely wanted to mention those who had passed on for fear of saying the wrong thing or upsetting someone.

Her voice shook slightly when she answered. "He was wonderful," she said softly. "My mother left us when I was tiny, and he brought me up on his own. He never moaned or let me think I was missing out on something. Everything he did was for me."

She added the chopped chicken to the lettuce and absentmindedly washed the chopping board before turning to grab the toasted ciabatta loaf.

"He was passionate about the local community and did lots of fundraising to help restore the church," she continued. "Everyone loved him."

"He sounds like an amazing guy," Jordan said. "He would be so proud of what you have built here."

Kat closed her eyes as if this simple action helped her recall all the moments she had shared with her father that had shaped who she was. He was always in her thoughts, but talking about him so openly brought so many memories to mind.

"There was an old guy called Ben who was in his eighties and lived on a rickety old barge near Mapleton village. Dad used to take him a bag of shopping once a week as Ben was a bit unsteady on his legs. One day, Dad dropped off Ben's groceries, but the old guy hadn't got his hearing aid in, so he didn't hear Dad climb on board. Ben got the fright of his life and knocked Dad into the canal with his sweeping brush."

She chuckled at the memory. "Dad looked like the swamp monster when he climbed out of the water."

Jordan smiled at her. "I bet you've got so many stories to share."

"Oh yes. A lot of my guests tell me I should write a book," she said with a wide smile.

"Would I feature?" he asked.

She looked up into Jordan's deep brown eyes and smiled. "Let me see how you handle cleaning out the compost toilet, and then we can talk about whether I include you in my book."

Jordan snorted and slapped his hand on the counter. "I reckon I can handle anything you throw at me, Captain."

"You need to survive my chicken Caesar salad first," she teased, sliding the bowl across the counter towards him.

"Cut!"

Kat jumped at Ted's loud instruction, almost forgetting there were other people on board.

"Perfect. Y'all are naturals, and judging by the comments left on Beth's videos from yesterday's trip, the fans are going to love this show."

Kat had sneaked a look at Beth's account the night before as she crawled into bed and watched herself light up when Jordan swept his arm wide to let her down the stone staircase at Warwick Castle. To the uneducated observer, it definitely came across like she and Jordan were the best of friends.

"This looks great," Jordan said, interrupting her thoughts as he tucked into his lunch.

The heat crept up Kat's face, and she turned away to fill the sink with water for washing up.

"Leave the washing-up, Kat," Ted said. "I want Jordan to do the dishes so we can see that your guests are hands-on and help with the day-to-day tasks."

She looked back at Jordan, who was shovelling toasted ciabatta into his mouth. "Enjoy your chores," she said with a wide smile.

"Oh, I will. Washing up is one of the first things you learn in acting school, isn't that right, Martha?"

Martha squeezed Kat's arm as she joined them in the kitchen. "It is indeed, and you were always top of your class."

The warm smile Jordan gave Martha dislodged something in Kat's chest. Despite the conversation she had had with Martha, and now knowing a little more of Jordan's backstory, her animosity towards him had thawed considerably. His mood swings were enough to give anyone whiplash, but the more time she spent with him, the more she saw his true nature. The media and his awful knack for getting into trouble were only a small part of Jordan Harrington's life. She was starting to enjoy peeling back the layers.

"Kat, can I get you outside for some exterior shots, please?" Ted said, sticking his head through the door. "Cole will make sure Jordan's washing-up is up to standard."

"Hell yes, I will," Cole said with a salute in Kat's direction, which made her chuckle. She took one last look at Jordan devouring his chicken and followed Ted outside.

Today's energy felt different. Even though Jordan hadn't yet learned the truth from Ted and Martha, it was almost like their argument, a fun day out with everyone, and the previous day's strange phone call and subsequent mood had rolled back the storm clouds and allowed the sunshine in.

They spent the next hour getting footage of Kat tying and untying ropes, washing the exterior windows, pottering with her herbs on the roof, chatting to a couple of people walking past, and pretending to talk on the phone to book a mooring spot.

Beth hovered in the background, grabbing shots of Ted and Cole filming Jordan and Kat, and turning them into reels.

It was only when they set off cruising that Kat had time to look at Beth's account and saw the snippets of interaction between her and Jordan over lunch. It looked like two friends laughing and enjoying one another's company. The comments were full of *'love these two'* and *'aww, how cute, they are adorable together'*.

The entire thing was staged; Kat knew that in her gut. Everything she was watching was intended to show the world, and the many casting directors, that Jordan Harrington was a nice guy worthy of consideration, but the way it looked almost convinced her that it was real.

She was about to stuff her phone back in her pocket when it rang. Paul's number flashed up and Kat's stomach flipped.

"Hello?"

"Kat, it's me. Can you talk?"

"Hi, yes, we're cruising at the moment, so I'm free for a bit. How are you?"

"I'm good, thanks. It looks like you're having fun with your film crew."

Kat wondered if Paul had been watching the footage and reading the comments on Beth's posts too and was a tiny bit jealous. Was that why he was calling her now?

"How can I help?" she said, trying to act uninterested.

"I was hoping you could meet me," he said. "You must be getting close to mooring near the King's Head, so I could drive out and buy you dinner."

Dinner. Kat couldn't deny the fact that her pulse quickened at the thought of seeing Paul again. Was he ready to admit he had been wrong? Was he watching her and the business getting pushed into the limelight and needed to apologise? Did he worry that she was getting involved with Jordan, as the staged footage seemed to imply?

"We'll reach the King's Head mooring about five o'clock today," she said. "I could meet you at the pub about seven."

"That's great," he said. "I'll see you later, Kat."

She hung up and texted Stephanie with an update. They hadn't spoken since before the half-naked women incident and Martha's revelation, and she knew there wouldn't be time to speak before tonight's meeting with Paul. The next phone call between them would need to be about four hours long, but what would she tell her friend? Would she be able to say Paul had come grovelling back?

★ ★ ★

The smell of Cajun spice filled the *Creaky Cauldron* as Kat got ready for her date with Paul. Jordan had announced he was cooking dinner, but Kat hadn't had the heart to tell him she was going out; not that she thought he would care if she was there or not.

She knew this newfound love of cooking was his way of apologising yet again. Martha had told her as much when they were tying up the boats earlier.

"He wants to make amends, but his pride sometimes gets in the way of actually saying the words 'I'm sorry'," she said. "He tries to show it in other ways, and cooking is one of his ways of apologising for all his moods and drama."

Kat felt a flutter of elation knowing that Jordan had been able to say he was sorry to her, but she also felt bad that it looked like she was rejecting his attempts to build bridges with her and the rest of the crew. Meeting Paul felt important to her. She wanted to listen to what he had to say and see if they could build their own bridges.

Although she knew Paul had acted like an ass over her business plan and dropping the 'let's take a break' on her, he had also promised to see her again. This was the ideal opportunity to clear the air. She could express her concerns and what she wanted in the future and he could explain what he needed from their relationship so they were mutually content.

Watching Jordan pivot from decent human to terse and moody wasn't what she wanted for herself and Paul. That type of relationship belonged to the rich and famous, and she was grateful they didn't have the same Hollywood dramas to contend with. This dinner would be the perfect time to reconnect.

Everyone was crowded into the living room of the *Creaky Cauldron* as Jordan busied himself in the kitchen, using every pot, pan, plate, and utensil she owned.

Cole let out a long, low whistle when she walked into the room. "You look hot as hell," he said. "Who's the lucky fella?"

Kat blushed and smoothed down her fitted dress. The nature of her life meant she didn't often get the opportunity to dress up, so she only had one or two good outfits. The royal blue dress had short sleeves, a low-cut cleavage, and stopped short of her knees, showing off her shapely calves. Thanks to the glorious sunshine, she could team it with silver ballet pumps and a matching bag.

"I'm having dinner with a friend," she said.

She had tried to avoid looking in Jordan's direction, although she knew he had stopped whatever he was doing and was watching her, like everyone else.

"But I've cooked." His voice wasn't much more than a whisper.

Kat's gaze lifted from the floor to his face. She didn't miss the disappointment etched into his features

"I know, I'm sorry. This is important; otherwise, I'd love to join you. It smells delicious." She rushed over her words, trying to cover up the nerves she felt about the evening and her unease over leaving Jordan thinking she didn't care about his gesture.

She gave him a wide smile. "If there's enough left, I'd love you to save me some."

Jordan nodded and turned back to the pan on the hob.

"Have a good night then," she said, forcing herself to sound as natural as possible despite the churning in her gut.

Beth knew where Kat was going in case there was an emergency on the boat and they needed to reach her, but she didn't volunteer her plans to anyone else as she closed the door behind her and walked down the footpath.

Looking back, she could see Jordan glancing at the closed door while the rest of them carried on their conversations. It was the first night she felt like she was missing out. Up until that moment, she had longed to escape the strange atmosphere on board by going to the local pub, but that night felt different.

She vowed to make it up to Jordan the next day and ensure he understood that she was okay about everything that had happened between them, even that night with the half-naked women. It felt important that he knew they were friends. Even thinking that felt odd, but when she thought about the small group sitting back in her living room, friends were exactly what she would call them.

Paul was already at the King's Head when she arrived. He had chosen a table in the beer garden alongside the brick wall on the perimeter, so they were more secluded. The climbing roses covered the walls, their tiny buds pouting in readiness to bloom.

"You look beautiful," he said when she appeared, giving her a tender kiss on the cheek before inviting her to sit down. "I'm so glad you came."

They ordered a round of drinks and a wood-fired

pizza, which the pub was well-known for, and made small talk until the food arrived.

"I'd forgotten how good these pizzas were," Kat said, tucking into her second slice.

"You always did enjoy your food." Paul laughed.

They chatted about his work, Tom's marketing for the business, and the warmer spring weather they were having, and she wondered if Paul would get to the point of their meeting.

"How are you getting on with the Americans?"

Finally. Kat pondered if by 'Americans' he meant Jordan.

"It's been an adjustment," she said. "But the crew are brilliant, and they've taken to life on the cut really well. Martha is a natural at navigating, and I've just left Jordan cooking up a storm in the kitchen."

She watched Paul's expression for any flicker of jealousy, but his face remained unreadable.

"That's great, Kat. It sounds like it's paid off for you then."

"Maybe you should have invested," she teased.

He laughed and excused himself to go buy another round of drinks.

American accents drifted across the beer garden, and Kat turned around to see Jordan, Cole, and Beth sitting down at one of the other tables. They were far enough away that she couldn't hear what they were saying, and in turn, they wouldn't be able to hear her and Paul, but she was mortified that they were there in the first place.

Paul returned with a large glass of red wine for her and

a pint of beer for himself. She took a large gulp in a bid to calm her nerves.

Why would Beth bring them here when she knew this was where Kat was going to be?

Trying to ignore them, she focused her attention on Paul. "You mentioned something about a promotion."

"Yes, it's a senior leadership role with a great salary."

"That's brilliant, Paul. You deserve it."

"I'm thrilled, but it also means a relocation."

Relocation. Was that why he wanted to meet? Did he hope to get back together but it all depended on the commute?

"Where are you going?"

"Sheffield," he said. "It's the company's head office where I'll be based, and I'll be leading one of the largest teams in the UK. I'm pretty excited about it."

She nodded along, with a smile plastered on her face as she did the travel maths. Sheffield wasn't that far from Warwickshire, probably only a couple of hours. Long-distance relationships worked all the time; they just needed to find a rhythm. Although Sheffield wasn't known for its waterways, she was sure they could figure something out.

"It's great, Paul. A new adventure sounds perfect."

Jordan's loud laugh carried across the beer garden, momentarily distracting her.

"Isn't that your Jordan Harrington?" Paul said.

She glanced over her shoulder and forced an 'oh' sound as if she hadn't noticed his arrival or existence.

"Yes, I thought they were all staying on board the boat tonight. His cooking must not have been a hit and they've had to come out for decent food. And he's not *my* Jordan Harrington, far from it."

"Do you want to join them?"

"God, no!" she said, a bit too aggressively. "I've come to have dinner with you and enjoy catching up. I spend all day, every day with that lot."

She looked back over her shoulder and Jordan caught her eye. He smiled and waved, which mortified her even more.

"If we ignore them, they might go away." She laughed.

"I thought you loved all your Floating Solo guests," Paul teased.

"Very funny. I'm used to *solo* travellers, not a mass invasion."

In truth, Kat loved all her guests, some more than others, but she didn't want Paul to think the sweet Instagram reels and gushing comments from Jordan's fans implied more than a host and guest relationship.

They chatted easily about Paul's new role and how much fun Kat was having with the crew and learning about filming. She told him about their day trip to Warwick Castle and the buzz it had created with a potential audience for Ted's show. They were four drinks down when Paul finally got to the point of them meeting up.

"There is something else I need to talk to you about," he said, pushing his pint to the side and taking hold of her hands.

Here it was. She knew it would take some organising, but she was certain that between them they could make the relocation and commute work. He had seen how much visibility her business was getting and the potential Floating Solo now had to allow for expansion and give them the opportunity to settle down.

"Kat, I'm…"

Jordan's laughter and loud voice pierced the air and she tutted.

"He keeps the entire canal awake all night with that mouth," she said, shaking her head.

Paul laughed and tightened his hold on her hands, glancing briefly at where Jordan, Cole, and Beth sat.

"Kat, I'm getting married."

Chapter Eleven

The world narrowed down until only their table in the corner of the beer garden existed. Kat heard the words but couldn't comprehend what they meant. Had she missed his proposal? Was he asking her to marry him but messed up how to ask?

"I know it's hard to hear, but I wanted the opportunity to explain so you understood."

She didn't understand.

"I met Rose about six months ago, and we got on well. I didn't mean for anything to happen between us, but neither of us could deny our feelings. She runs her own business so she can work remotely, which fits in with my move to Sheffield perfectly."

Kat watched his lips moving and could hear the words, but her entire focus was on his hands still holding hers. She ripped them away in sudden disgust.

"I didn't want you to find out from someone else," he said, trying to reach for her again. "Stephanie was right. It needed to come from me."

Stephanie.

Kat suddenly felt lightheaded. Stephanie *knew* about Paul's deceit and hadn't said anything. Is that what Tom was referring to before she started this trip? He asked

Stephanie if she had told Kat something, but it had been swept away, and she assumed it was about her illness. Or perhaps it was when they had bumped into Paul in town, which would explain Stephanie's strange tone on the phone when she asked if Paul had been in touch. Either way, her best friend had known and hadn't told her.

The burning pain in her chest wasn't a new sensation. She had felt it before, standing in front of a mirror getting her wedding dress altered when her then fiancé walked in and told her it was over, two weeks before the wedding. The sensation was what she imagined having her heart ripped out of her chest would feel like. It was the worst pain she had ever experienced and signalled the end of her trusting anyone again. She had lowered her armour enough to let Paul inside, only to discover he was as bad as everyone else, but Stephanie, whom she had known for many years, was supposed to be the one person she could rely on. She thought she could trust her friends, but it now seemed that even they had let her down.

How could she?

The pain in her chest intensified. Tears streamed down her face, and she frantically swiped at them with the back of her hand. She didn't want Paul to see her so upset, but the tears refused to stop.

"Don't cry, Kat. It's not personal."

Not personal. She laughed through the tears.

"Of course it's personal, Paul," she hissed. "You're telling me this Rose woman can work from anywhere and be with you in Sheffield when I've been breaking my back trying to build my own business so we can do the same.

And then you casually drop in that you've been sleeping with this woman for six months when we only broke up recently."

All Kat could focus on was the red mist that seemed to swirl around her and the deep wave of anger tearing through her body. Her voice got louder with every word until Paul's eyes were anxiously flicking across the beer garden at the people staring over.

She stood, picked up her wine glass, and threw the contents in Paul's face.

"Fuck you, fuck Rose, and fuck your pretentious life," she forced out between pursed lips before grabbing her bag and storming out of the beer garden.

She was fully aware that the entire outside area had gone deathly quiet, and all eyes were on her, but she was beyond caring. The fact that Jordan was one of those gobsmacked onlookers mildly irritated her, but right now, all she wanted was to run away and forget Paul, Rose, Stephanie, Jordan, and the entire world existed.

The *Creaky Cauldron* was her safe space, but when she unlocked the door and went inside, a stack of dirty pans, plates, and glasses greeted her. The kitchen looked like a war zone, with Cajun sauce stuck to the worktop and down the front of the cabinets.

She ignored the mess and went for the unopened bottle of red wine, unscrewing the top and drinking straight from the bottle. Sliding down the side of the sofa, she dropped to the floor and sobbed. Nothing would stop the tears. She cried, drank, and cried some more.

It didn't take her long to drain the bottle of wine, and as

she opened the cabinet to find a second bottle, on the shelf she spotted a framed photo of her and Paul at Stephanie's birthday party a couple of years ago. They were laughing together with Paul's arm draped affectionately around Kat's shoulders. That was the night he first told her he loved her.

She plucked it off the shelf and hurled it across the room, the glass shattering into a million pieces against the wall on impact. As the tears began falling once again, the door to the *Creaky Cauldron* opened and Jordan stepped inside.

"No, no, no, you need to leave," Kat slurred. "Sleep with the others tonight. I can't have you here."

She waved her hands in the air as if stopping traffic, but Jordan ignored her and slowly walked across the living room to where she stood by the open cabinet and the multiple bottles of wine. He shut the cabinet and stood in front of her.

"Get out!" she yelled. "Leave me alone."

"I'm not going anywhere, Kat."

Hearing him say her name so softly broke something inside her and she collapsed, sobbing hysterically. Jordan caught her and lowered her to the floor, slipping his arms around her in a protective bubble so she could bury her face in his chest and cry.

He didn't say a word or ask her to talk, just held her while she let it all out, and when she exhausted herself, he scooped her up and carried her to bed, covering her with the blankets and kissing her forehead, which made her cry again.

"Thank you," she whispered.

He nodded, lingering in the doorway for a moment, and then shut the door, leaving her in the dark with her thoughts and her overwhelming sadness.

★ ★ ★

When Kat opened her eyes the next morning, her initial reaction was to groan at the pounding in her head, then the thought of cleaning the kitchen, followed by the difficult conversation she needed to have with Stephanie. At no point did she want to revisit what had happened with Paul.

Swinging her legs out of bed, she realised the boat was in motion. She flicked open the curtain to see the hedgerows gently sweeping past as the *Creaky Cauldron* meandered down the canal. Who the hell was steering?

The tiller was situated at the back of the boat and accessed through her bedroom, but if someone wanted to set off without disturbing the occupant, they could climb aboard from the towpath. Opening the back door, she was shocked to see Jordan standing to the right of the tiller, leaning against the back railing. He looked like he had been boating all his life.

"Good morning," he said, glancing down at her as she stuck her head outside.

Jordan had dropped her into bed fully clothed, so she was still wearing her blue dress from the night before.

"There's a chill in the air this morning, so you might need a sweater," he said.

Mumbling to herself, she backed away and closed the door behind her. Jordan Harrington was steering the boat by himself. Had he been taking notice of her lessons this entire time?

She grabbed a pair of jeans from her wardrobe and a dark red hoodie, dressed, and wandered into the kitchen. If Jordan was happy playing captain outside, she would tackle the mess he had left inside.

For a moment, Kat thought she must have dreamt the overflowing pots and pans in the sink and the remains of dinner smeared across her kitchen cupboards, because the galley sparkled. Everything was in its place, and the worksurface was clear and clean. Even the broken photo frame and shattered glass were gone, and a steaming pot of coffee and a clean mug were waiting for her, alongside a glass of water and a couple of aspirin.

She couldn't stop the tremble of her bottom lip or the tears that tumbled down her face. In fact, she hadn't even thought it was possible to cry any more tears after the previous night, and yet here they were.

Perhaps the man who ridiculed everyone, disrespected her, and was moody and irritable all the time wasn't the asshole she had originally thought.

She was about to go join Jordan outside to thank him when her phone buzzed in her pocket and Stephanie's number flashed up.

Stephanie was her best friend and had been a big support to her in so many ways, but could she have a civil conversation with her without screaming at her for keeping such a huge secret?

"Hello." Her tone was cold as she answered the phone.

"Hey, are you okay?" Stephanie asked.

"Not even a little bit."

There was a long silence on the other end before Stephanie spoke. "I assume you've spoken to Paul."

"Last night."

Another long pause. Kat didn't have it in her to deal with long sentences, and it was taking all her strength to keep a lid on her bubbling emotions. Tears were welling up once more, and she didn't want to start crying again.

"I'm so sorry I didn't tell you, Kat. Paul's a wanker, and I didn't want to give him the satisfaction of not telling you himself. It would have been the easy way out for him to have me tell you what was going on. You deserve better than that."

Kat knew her friend was speaking the truth. Stephanie would have softened the blow with her usual support and even made her feel better about it all with humour and snacks.

"I threw a glass of wine in his face," she said softly. "In front of everyone in the King's Head beer garden."

Stephanie laughed, which melted some of the ice that coated Kat's heart.

"That's my girl." she said. "I'm truly sorry. Tom took me into town for an appointment with the doctor, and we saw Paul with his other woman, and…"

"I don't need to know the details," Kat said. "He's a lying, cheating bastard, but at least he'll be those things in a different county soon."

She sipped her coffee before running over Stephanie's words in her mind. "Doctor? Why did you have to go back to the doctor? Are you still sick?"

"I'm still queasy, but the doctor got to the bottom of it," Stephanie gushed. "It turns out the reason I've been so tired and sick is because I'm pregnant."

Kat squealed. "Omigod, Steph! That's amazing news. I'm so happy for you both."

All the hurt and sadness Paul had inflicted was instantly washed away. Stephanie and Tom had been trying for years to have a baby without any luck. They were saving up for IVF treatment and had almost reached their goal, but now it looked like the money they had saved could be used to provide for the baby's arrival.

"When? What is it? How?" Her questions tumbled out one after the other, and they both laughed.

"We had no idea. I'd pretty much given up hope and was busy saving rather than tracking my cycle," she said. "The doctor said I'm about twelve weeks along, so we're due in early December. I'm not going to find out what we're having, as we both want it to be a surprise, and I hope you don't actually need me to tell you *how* it happened."

"Oh, blimey, no, I don't need details. I've got Fifty Shades on Netflix for that."

"We wanted to ask if you'd be the baby's godmother, Kat. Will you? Please say yes."

The tears started falling once more, but this time, they were happy tears.

"I'd be honoured, thank you."

"You'll make a great godmother. Now, we're going to have lots of time to talk about babies when you get home soon, so spill. I want all the juicy gossip from the canal. What's our moody hero been like lately?"

Kat felt her face flush, and as she looked around her clean kitchen, she realised her sudden shift in opinion might confuse Stephanie as much as it did her. The last time they spoke, she had told her how awful Jordan was and how she was counting down the days until she could kick him off the boat. Now, the thought of him, or any of them, going home left a hole in her chest.

"Well, there was the half-naked women in my living room, the Cajun sauce up my cupboards, and him carrying me to bed, but other than that, nope, nothing much to report."

It was Stephanie's turn to squeal down the phone as Kat settled into her comfy armchair and filled her in on every small detail of the last few days.

★ ★ ★

As they moored up for the night on a quiet stretch of canal, it occurred to Kat they had done barely any filming that day.

When she had eventually relieved Jordan at the tiller, he disappeared inside for a few hours and then joined the other boat after lunch. From her position further along the canal, Kat could see Cole with his camera and Beth capturing her iconic real-life footage, but all the crew had kept their distance from Kat and the *Creaky Cauldron* all day.

Although it was exactly what she needed, she didn't want the team to think she was fragile and needed a break.

Kat was tugging on the mooring rope to check it was tight when Martha strolled up to her.

"Everything okay, Kat?"

How she asked made Kat fully aware that Jordan had filled her in on the previous night's explosive evening. Her only hope was that Beth hadn't caught it on her phone.

"Sore head, puffy eyes, and exhausted to my bones, but apart from that, I'm okay. I take it Jordan told you what happened."

Martha nodded and linked her arm with hers as they walked towards the bow of the *Creaky Cauldron*.

"He told me basic details about your meeting at the pub, but he didn't say much more."

Another tick in the box for Jordan Harrington.

"Beth is mortified that she convinced Jordan and Cole to go with her to the same pub you were at and witness the unfortunate events," Martha continued. "I don't think she grasped the severity of the situation."

"She's sweet, and I know she only meant well. I'd told her where I was going in case anyone needed me, but I didn't give her *all* the facts. I might have kept a few of the finer details to myself."

"So she thought she was getting a ringside seat to your dating life. Instead, she caused you more upset by providing an audience."

"It's not Beth who upset me. Far from it. Paul, the guy I met at the pub, was my boyfriend until recently. I thought he wanted to meet me to get back together, but he actually wanted to tell me he'd been seeing someone else and they're getting married."

Martha made a small, strangled sound and shook her head so hard Kat thought her teeth might fall out.

"What is the matter with young men these days? They have a beautiful woman by their side, but they act like ignorant idiots."

"Are you married?" Kat asked, trying to remember if she'd seen a wedding ring on Martha's finger.

"No, I don't have time for any of that nonsense," Martha said, waving her free hand in the air. "Ted keeps me busy."

A thought suddenly occurred to Kat. "Is Ted married?" she asked with a sly smile.

"Don't start waving your cupid wings in our direction." Martha chuckled. "Ted has been single for as long as I have. We might act like an old married couple, but we're colleagues and good friends, nothing more."

Kat couldn't deny feeling a little bit disappointed by that news. Martha and Ted acted like the group's parents, so it went without saying that they should be getting the perks of being a couple.

"What about Cole and Beth? Any developments in that department yet?"

Martha raised her eyebrows as they sat on the bench seats. "So, it's you that planted that seed, is it? Cole and Beth do seem to be getting along, and I wondered why this was happening all of a sudden when they've worked together for over a year."

"It's painfully obvious that Cole is smitten; he just needed a gentle nudge."

"I happen to agree with you, but it's not them I want to talk about. It's you."

"Me? Is there something wrong with the trip?"

"Not at all. Kat, I wanted to check you were okay and to see if you needed a break from us for a while."

She *had* been right. Everyone *had* gone out of their way to avoid her today.

"I guessed that Jordan would say something, and I appreciated not having a camera stuck in my face today," she said, pointing at the puffy eyes. "But I'm okay. In fact, I'm almost relieved. It's like everything that was holding me back has been released."

Martha reached forward and patted Kat's hand in that motherly way some older women have, leaving you feeling understood and supported.

"It often happens that way," Martha said. "The one thing or person you thought was important ends up being what keeps you down. Breaking free of this man and his lies will set you on a new path, and that can open up a lot of opportunities for you. In fact, I wanted to talk to you about something that could be beneficial to us both, but I've got to fly back to the US for a few days to see my uncle. Can we chat when I get back?"

"Of course. I'd like that," Kat said, her mind working overtime as she tried to think what Martha could possibly suggest for their mutual benefit. "Is everything okay with your uncle?"

It was one hell of a commute for Martha to take for a few days, but then she assumed travelling long haul at the drop of a hat was a regular occurrence for those in Martha's industry.

"He's not been good recently, and he took a turn for the worse yesterday. I need to check he's got all the care and support he needs. My uncle is like a father to me, so it's important I go. I'll be craving this slow pace and fresh air when I get back."

"You'll be exhausted, Martha. Wouldn't it be better if we paused the trip to give you more time?"

"Not at all. I'm used to living out of a cabin bag. I'll be gone for four days, max."

"Okay, if you're sure. Don't worry about a thing. I'll look after everyone until you get back."

"I hope that everyone looks after you too," Martha said with a warm smile.

As Martha headed off to grab the overnight bag Beth was holding out for her, Kat realised Martha was the glue that stuck the group together. The dynamics would no doubt change when she was away, but Kat vowed to help keep Ted on schedule, support Cole, and Beth the best she could, and repay Jordan for his kindness.

Chapter Twelve

Since the unfortunate event in the King's Head beer garden three nights earlier, Jordan Harrington had morphed into one of the *Creaky Cauldron*'s most well-behaved guests.

Kat was used to letting everyone have a go at the various daily tasks necessary to keep a narrowboat in good working order, but Jordan seemed to know what needed doing before she could ask.

Filming was becoming a joy as she began to relax around him. She almost didn't notice when Cole and Ted were around as Jordan made her feel at ease. It felt like a normal Floating Solo holiday.

"I can see the appeal of travelling at four miles an hour now," Jordan said as he stood at the tiller early the next morning. Kat was spending less time steering these days, which meant she was on hand to help Beth navigate *Dreamcatcher* in Martha's absence, but this morning, Cole had volunteered to help Beth until they moored for lunch.

"I'm glad the waterways are winning you over." She giggled. "Life is so much better in slow motion."

Jordan adjusted his sunglasses so they sat on top of his head. He looked like one of those handsome models in cologne advertisements.

"There aren't many opportunities in LA to enjoy anything in slow motion."

"Not even the traffic jams?" she teased.

He chuckled. "The traffic might be slow, but it's still a chaotic frenzy with all the horns blaring and the drivers screaming at each other."

"Blimey, the loudest scream you'll find out here is a goat in a field."

Jordan laughed, and she marvelled at how attractive he was when he wasn't scowling. She liked his smile and the way his cheeks dipped in slightly. Lately, she had been struggling to remember what she didn't like about him.

Since Martha had rushed off to care for her uncle, Jordan had stepped up and been more hands-on and helpful. He cooked more, cleaned everything, and she even found him helping fix a puncture for a cyclist on the towpath when they stopped the previous night.

"Are you feeling better now?"

Jordan's question came out of nowhere and surprised her.

"What do you mean?" she asked. She knew full well what he was referring to, but she needed to prepare herself for having that conversation. She had managed to gloss over it with Stephanie, who was her dearest friend, so she couldn't imagine how it would feel to hash it all out with a Hollywood star.

"The man at the pub. I'm assuming that was *the* boyfriend."

"*Was*, yes. He came to tell me he's marrying the woman he's been seeing behind my back for the past six months."

She couldn't disguise the bitterness in her voice.

"Woah, that's heavy. He deserved more than a drink in the face."

Kat smiled at the memory. She had taken great pride in embarrassing Paul in public, even though she had wasted a perfectly good drink.

"I improvised with what I had."

"We'll make an actor out of you yet," Jordan chuckled.

The silence stretched out, but it wasn't uncomfortable, more like they were both processing their thoughts before speaking again. She was about to open her mouth when Jordan spoke up.

"I've bounced from one bad relationship to another," he said, not taking his eyes off the canal and the front of the boat. "I have a bad habit of attracting drama wherever I go."

Kat wasn't sure what to say. She had read so many articles about Jordan and the string of gorgeous girlfriends, but how much of it was true?

"You and Lexi seem to be back together and doing okay," she said finally, although from what Martha had told her and the dark clouds that swept over his face whenever he looked at his phone, that was yet another bad relationship hurtling towards its fiery end. Kat wanted to know if Jordan knew that or if he was smitten, like Cole with Beth.

He didn't answer at first, and she thought he either hadn't heard her or chose to ignore the question, until finally he responded.

"We broke up," he said, slipping his glasses back on

and running his hand through his hair. He adjusted his stance as if sharing that news had revealed his greatest vulnerabilities and he was preparing to run for his life.

Kat laid her hand on his arm as he gripped the tiller, feeling the need to comfort him in some small way. What he had done for her the other night played over and over in her mind and her simple action felt far too lame.

"I'm sorry to hear that." In truth, she wasn't sorry at all, but she knew it was only polite to commiserate in these situations.

"Don't be; she's the same as everyone else. Lexi was only with me for what it got her. Martha was always trying to tell me how toxic she was, but I didn't want to believe it, even though the evidence was piling up around me. Did you know she only landed her contract on that Netflix show after I made a few calls? She wasn't getting work and was stressing out about it, so I helped her out. Now I'm the one without any work, and all she can do is badmouth me all over social media."

He removed his sunglasses and tucked the arm into his T-shirt so they hung like a necklace at his throat. He glanced over at Kat, his eyes searching her face as if to see if the news shocked her.

"Martha told you?" he said eventually. "That nobody wants to work with me."

Kat nodded. "I'm so sorry, Jordan; she mentioned it was the reason behind the docuseries when I hounded her about Beth's behind-the-scenes videos." She wanted it to seem like Martha had had no choice but to tell her rather than his trusted agent speaking out of turn.

"It's okay. I guess everyone knew except me." His shoulders slumped as he half laughed, half humphed. It sounded like all the air in his lungs had suddenly left his body. He shook his head before speaking again. "I think somewhere, deep down, I did know but didn't want to believe it."

"I think being here might change everyone's views," Kat said, trying to find the words to make him feel better. This was Stephanie's area of expertise. "The comments Beth is getting on her videos are really positive. A casting agent will see how funny, amazing, and handsome you are and snap you up."

His sidelong glance was full of mischief and the corner of his mouth twitched into a smile at her words. "You think I'm handsome?"

The heat rushed up Kat's cheeks and she turned away from him before he could see her squirm.

"Go on, we're trying to big me up and lift my mood, so you can tell me I'm handsome again; I don't mind."

Kat laughed and nudged into him, making the tiller move and the boat judder.

"Hey, when did I become the one who could drive the boat better than you?" he teased.

"Drive! Oh yes, I forgot. You don't drive boats, do you?"

"Okay, I admit it," Jordan said with a wink and a sexy half-smile. "I was an ass when we met. I'd had another huge fight with Lexi over the phone and I may have taken it out on everyone else, including you."

"Including me? I'd say especially me. I'd never wanted

to throw a guest overboard before you arrived, but I accept your explanation. Besides, I got to bitch about you with my best friend, so you gave us lots to gossip about."

His mock speechless expression made her laugh even louder.

"Don't worry, Stephanie's great at the whole psychology thing and working out why you are the way you are. She was the one who told me to invest in more boats and expand my Floating Solo business. She'll have you figured out in ten minutes."

"Great. Book me in with her for when we get back. Joking aside, I mentioned to Ted that I might need to talk to a counsellor when we get back to LA."

Their light-hearted banter shifted slightly as the clouds broke and the sun beat down on them. Jordan slid his sunglasses back on again, and Kat suddenly missed seeing his eyes. He kept his emotions in check, but she could always see the laughter and the pain reflected in his eyes.

"Talking therapies are powerful. Stephanie told me that, when I was looking for a counsellor after my dad died. It can be helpful to talk when you're brave enough to ask for the help you need."

"Exactly, and I have so much buried in here—" he thumped his fist to his chest "—that I worry it'll stop me being myself. It's like something is holding me back."

Kat remembered her conversation with Martha about the relief she felt over Paul leaving her life for good. Maybe that's what Jordan needed too. A clean slate.

"I didn't know my father," Jordan continued. "Ted is the closest thing I've had to the real thing. My mum was so busy raising my younger brothers and sisters with her second husband that she never had time for me. I got into all kinds of trouble."

His voice was soft as he reminisced, and Kat didn't dare breathe too loudly in case it broke the spell. Hearing him open up warmed her heart, and she wanted to learn more about the real Jordan Harrington, not the made-up version from the glossy magazines.

"Did you know it was Martha who found me and cleaned me up?"

"No, I didn't. I remember Ted telling me she found you modelling at a charity event or something."

"That's right, but I was there to score some drugs from a dodgy bloke who ran the venue. One of the charity guys saw me and asked me to step in as a model. Martha came looking for me after the show and chased the dealer away." He chuckled as he recalled the memory. "She's such a badass."

"She cares about you, all of you. I've watched the way you all interact with each other over the past week, and you're like a big happy family. It's nice to see, and I hadn't realised how much I've missed that."

"You're part of the family now, Kat."

She wanted to believe him, but they came from two different worlds. They were nearly halfway through the trip, and once they moored up at the marina in another week, all this would end. Her new family would leave, and she would be floating solo once more.

★ ★ ★

The bright stars filled the sky as Kat drank a mug of hot chocolate on the deck, wrapped up in a blanket. Jordan, Cole, and Beth had gone off to explore the local restaurants and bars, but Kat craved some alone time.

Her candid conversation with Jordan had struck a chord with her, and thoughts of finding a partner, settling down, and having a family whirled through her mind. Stephanie and Tom were going to become parents, and although she was overjoyed for her friends, she was also a little bit jealous.

Paul, for all his faults, wanted a simple life – a wife, a home, and a good job. Why couldn't she want something similar? Or was she destined to become the next Ben, a lonely old soul living on a barge while some kind villager fetched her weekly shopping?

Building her business was still the goal that excited her, but having someone to get excited with came a close second.

She sipped her hot chocolate and rested her head back so she could stare at the stars. There were no streetlights on the canal, and the darkness made the heavens sparkle. A slight breeze ruffled her hair, and she recalled there was a weather warning in place towards the end of the week. Right now, though, the late spring evening was pleasant, and she wanted to make the most of it.

Her phone vibrated, and she saw a text from Jordan. When she clicked on the message, a video popped up of him and Cole singing karaoke. She giggled and hit reply.

'You'll be inundated with offers for musicals if Beth shares this online. I can feel a remake of Les Mis on the horizon!'

She was happy they were enjoying themselves, although she didn't know if she would be able to show her face at quite a few of her regular establishments once the docuseries aired.

Smiling to herself, she locked the door and made her way to bed. The days seemed to be going faster and faster with the grand finale on the horizon. A deep sadness flooded through her at the thought of saying goodbye to Jordan and the rest of the crew, but that was something she would deal with when it came.

Although her bones felt weary, sleep eluded her. The gentle lapping of the water against the hull was usually enough to help her drift off, but that night her mind refused to switch off.

She had heard Jordan return an hour earlier and appreciated him trying to stay quiet, but even his movements, however silent, were magnified in the darkness.

Sick of tossing and turning, Kat threw the covers back on her bed and made her way to the kitchen for a glass of water. She didn't need to turn on any lights as she knew every inch of space inside the boat, and the moon was full enough to cast its creamy glow over everything. With a glass in hand she sat on the sofa, hoping that a change of environment would break the insomnia. A sound made her jump, and she almost screamed at the sight of someone looming over the side of the seat.

"Christ! Jordan, what the hell are you doing?"

Jordan jumped back and slammed his palm against his chest. "I didn't see you there," he said, running his other hand through his messy bed hair. "I heard a noise and thought I'd left the door unlocked."

Kat uncurled her legs and stood up, placing the empty glass on the side table. She was acutely aware that all she had on was a vest top and tiny sleep shorts, and Jordan was standing in front of her in his underwear.

"Sorry, I didn't mean to wake you up," she said, looking anywhere but at the contours of Jordan's chest in the pale glow shed by the moon.

"It's fine. I'm a light sleeper anyway."

They locked eyes for a long moment, and Kat felt the connection deep in her gut. If she didn't leave the room now, she might not be able to stop herself from saying or doing something she could regret.

"Well, goodnight then." She brushed past him on her way back towards her room, but he reached out for her and let his fingers trail over the skin on her arm. It was the lightest of touches, but it lit her skin up as if the moon had been dialled up to max.

"Kat, wait," he replied in a voice so soft it was almost a whisper.

Her limbs felt heavy and her legs refused to move even though she knew she should have already walked away and closed the bedroom door behind her. Instead, every nerve in her body was tingling with anticipation.

They were standing together in the mouth of the short corridor with the living space behind them and the bedrooms in front. Neither made the first move.

She could smell the sweet scent of aftershave on his skin mixed with the woody scents of the shower gel he liked to use. He took a small step towards her, and all the hairs on her neck stood to attention. His hands gently caressed her lower arms as he moved up to her elbows and then to her shoulders. She was finding it hard to catch her breath as his touch consumed her.

She leaned forward slightly as Jordan bent his head and touched his lips to hers. The kiss was soft and warm, tender even, and she melted into him. The kisses deepened as he pressed against her, his hands cupping her face and holding her steady, or was he holding her up? There was a strong possibility that she would crumple to the ground if he let go.

Jordan's hands moved from her face to explore her body, curling around her waist and pulling her closer still. There was no space between them, and yet he was eager to bring her nearer. Crushed up against him, she tried to catch her breath. His kisses were deep and intense, and it felt like an electrical current was running down her spine, which startled her. She had never been kissed like this before.

Tentatively, she ran her hands up his muscular arms, taking her time to feel the firm curvature of his biceps. She swept her hands up his neck and buried her fingers into the softness of his hair. His slight growl flipped her stomach alarmingly as she carefully trailed her fingernails down his chest and towards the waistband of his boxers.

His tongue explored her mouth as his hands cupped her bottom and lifted her from the floor, her legs wrapping neatly around him. With little effort, he carried her to her bedroom and set her down on the bed, his lips moving to her neck and shoulder.

"Kat," he moaned into her ear, and she thought her heart might explode. "Do you want to?"

Part of her wanted to laugh at such a ridiculous question. The way her body was responding to him should have given him a clear indication of the answer.

"Yes," she breathed. "I want to."

He reached for the straps of her vest top and slid them over her shoulders, kissing the bare flesh and moving his lips towards the swell of her breasts. As he tugged at the fabric revealing her taut nipples, she gasped, enjoying the soft moan that escaped him as he licked and sucked. Paul had never been so attentive nor gentle; his lovemaking was yet another task on his schedule. As Jordan nuzzled her neck with his warm kisses, she pushed all thoughts of Paul out of her mind. She wanted to be fully in this moment.

Running her hands down over Jordan's chest again, she inched closer to the top of his boxers, trailing a finger along the edge of the waistband until she had the courage to slide her hand inside. He moaned, louder this time, as Kat wrapped her fingers around him.

Jordan tugged at her sleep shorts, pulling them free and tossing them aside. His hands slowly travelled back up her legs as he continued to cover her body with kisses until he slid his fingers between her legs. Kat inhaled sharply, overcome with desire and the myriad of sensations that were flooding her body.

They explored each other's bodies, stroking, kissing, back and forth like the ocean's tide. There was an urgency to their movements, both aroused and desperate for the touches and caresses.

She pushed at his chest until they changed position and she was straddling him. In one movement, he lifted her vest top, tugging it over her head and discarding it on the floor. His strong hands swept up her back, pulling her to him as their kisses deepened.

"You're so beautiful," Jordan whispered into her ear as he flipped her onto her back and pushed himself deep inside her. His rhythm built to a crescendo that roared inside Kat's head. She wanted him to fill her up with joy and pleasure, and she never wanted him to stop.

Chapter Thirteen

The bright sunshine streaming through the curtains woke Kat, and for the briefest of moments, she forgot where she was.

Her body ached in a good way, and she swept her hands over her naked breasts, smiling at the memory of Jordan's hands doing the same thing the night before. She looked to her side, but the bed was empty. She hadn't heard him leave after their lovemaking, exhausted by the ferocity and passion they shared.

Grabbing her jeans and a T-shirt, she wandered down to the galley and living area, but Jordan was nowhere to be seen. His own bunk was empty.

A deep sense of foreboding settled in her gut as the enormity of what they had done hit her. Jordan wasn't like everyone else. He was a movie star destined for great things and a glitzy LA life. What the hell had she been thinking? They were from two different worlds.

It was early, and *Dreamcatcher* was still locked up with its curtains closed. The crew was sleeping, oblivious to Kat's sudden turmoil. She had no idea what she would say to Jordan when he did reappear. Maybe he was so mortified by what happened between them that he had slept on the floor of *Dreamcatcher* again.

Kat grabbed her phone and dialled Stephanie's number. If anyone could talk her off a ledge, it was her best friend.

"You're up early." Stephanie's voice sounded almost impressed. "Want to join my morning meditation?"

Kat chose to skip the chit-chat and friendly formality and blurted everything out in a rush of words.

"I slept with Jordan and it was the best sex I've ever had and now he's missing."

"Holy shit! First of all, breathe. Let me hear your deep breaths; come on."

Kat took a grounding breath in through her nose and released it through her mouth so Stephanie could hear her doing as she was told. She repeated the action three times and had to admit she did feel a bit calmer.

"Good, good, now tell me what happened. Slowly."

"We've been getting along recently, which is nice, but last night, we bumped into each other in the middle of the night, and one thing led to another."

Kat could almost hear her friend trying not to laugh.

"It's not funny, Stephanie. It's not right to cross the line with a guest, and *this* guest happens to be a bloody superstar."

Stephanie did laugh then. "Listen, anyone watching the behind-the-scenes footage would not be surprised by this news; in fact, they'd celebrate it. I promise you, it's what the entire internet wants. So you slept with Jordan Harrington, big deal."

"Big deal! I'm freaking out here, Stephanie; he's gorgeous and sexy as hell, and omigod, does he know how to navigate in the bedroom? But he's also here to get his life back on track. His boss is paying me to look after him, for Christ's sake."

"I wonder if you'll get a bonus for going above and beyond with looking after him." Stephanie couldn't restrain herself and burst into fits of laughter.

"I'm so glad my pain and drama are amusing for you," Kat grumbled.

"Don't worry. Jordan might not even mention it to the rest of them, so it can be your dirty little secret. You could get a bumper sticker with 'What happens on the *Creaky Cauldron*, stays on the *Creaky Cauldron*' printed."

A niggling thought sent a chill down Kat's spine.

"Oh no. Cole fitted cameras in the boat to capture us cooking and doing normal day-to-day tasks. What if they're constantly filming and caught it all on camera?"

"Jeez, Kat, you're going to be a porn star."

There was no stopping Stephanie's laughter. She tried to carry on the conversation but was gasping for breath at the end of the phone.

"You'll go into extra early labour if you keep laughing that hard," Kat said, her lip twitching into a smile at the sound of her friend's joy, even if it was at her own expense.

"At least you'll have a video memento of Jordan when he goes back to the States next week. Is there a camera in your bedroom?"

"Thankfully no, only the kitchen and living room, but one of them is angled, so it'll probably catch any movement in the corridor."

"Oh, Kat, you really do make me smile. Only you could have a fling with a Hollywood star. Wait till I tell Tom."

"Don't you dare. He'll end up making a reel about it or something equally mortifying."

"He wouldn't do that to you, although your new friends Beth and Cole might. What are you going to do?"

"Until I see Jordan and gauge his mood, I have no idea."

"It'll be okay, Kat. I promise. Read all the comments on the videos and posts that Beth has shared and that'll cheer you up. There is a lot of love for you guys, and everyone thinks your chemistry is fabulous. The entire internet can't be wrong, so maybe there is a happy ending for you."

Kat thanked Stephanie and ended the call, stuffing her phone back into her jeans and flipping on the kettle. She needed a strong coffee to tackle the day.

Maybe Stephanie was right and Jordan would realise the slow and simple life was much more appealing. Yeah, who was she kidding?

The door opened, making her jump, and Jordan ducked his tall body under the frame and placed two takeaway coffee cups on the side.

"You read my mind," Kat said, reaching to take the one he slid across the counter to her. "I can't function without my coffee in the morning."

She watched his movements and the expressions that constantly danced across his handsome face, but he was giving nothing away.

"I'm sorry about last night," he said finally. "I took advantage of you. It won't happen again." His voice was clipped and not full of the warmth she had got used to over the last couple of days.

"You know what my track record is like when it comes to women," he continued. "I only ever end up hurting people, and I can't add you to that list. I let myself get carried away, and it was wrong."

List. Kat's head began spinning, but she tried to focus on the heat of the takeaway cup and the strong taste of coffee as it passed her lips.

"You're my host, and I was unprofessional. I'm truly sorry. I won't tell Ted about this, if that's okay with you, as I don't want him to think our involvement will impact filming."

Involvement. List. Host. Wrong. Unprofessional.

The words whirled around Kat's brain like a load of dirty washing on its final spin setting. She had prepared herself for a moment or two of awkward silence until they were able to laugh it off or have an adult conversation, but not that. Nothing could have prepared her for that.

He grabbed his coffee and retreated outside muttering something about checking if Cole was awake yet. Kat placed the coffee cup on the counter and took a slow, deep breath in and out, pinching the bridge of her nose with her free hand as she relished the space and silence.

The resentment began to rise from her gut as she realised she was nothing more than another notch on Jordan Harrington's bedpost. Maybe she was his first British fling, or he wanted to make Lexi jealous. It didn't matter what the entire internet wanted; everything was a lie. The docuseries was fake, as was the behind-the-scenes set-up. All staged to try to revive an actor's flagging career. How had she been so stupid as to let her guard down around a man like Jordan Harrington?

It also didn't matter that she knew more about his history and family or that their recent conversations revolved around his desire to be a better man. Had all that been for the camera? Stephanie was probably right and Ted would use the steamy footage from the previous night as part of the marketing package to sell Jordan as the perfect actor to cast in the next romance blockbuster.

How quickly thoughts and emotions shifted. The night before, Kat was sad because the days were going so fast, and yet now, she was back to counting down the days until she was free of Jordan Harrington once again.

★ ★ ★

Kat's dream of a fleet of Floating Solo boats seemed further away than ever as she stood by the tiller, navigating the boat along the canal. The grey skies and rain that had been forecast had arrived with gusto and battered the boats, matching her mood perfectly.

They only had about half an hour of cruising before reaching the mooring for the night, so she pushed on. The rain was unpleasant, but she wanted to be set up and fixed firmly for the night before the winds began. Navigating a narrowboat in strong winds was enough to turn any seasoned boater's hair grey.

Once they arrived, she would need to teach the crew how to secure the boats so they could ride out the storm. Part of her hoped that Jordan would choose to stay on *Dreamcatcher* when they hunkered down and waited for the bad weather to pass. He had apologised to her over and over as if a simple 'sorry' made all the hurt, pain, and shame disappear, but he didn't understand how much he had turned her world upside down. Jordan was used to random dalliances, one-night stands, and casual sex, but that wasn't something *she* valued. She needed more, and from their conversations, she had foolishly believed that he needed more too.

She felt so disconnected from everything. There was a heavy weight lodged in her chest, and she struggled to be normal around him. He had had years of practice wearing a mask for the camera, but she didn't have the same skill set. Snapping at him came easier than trying to move past the pain in her heart.

"Is there something wrong?" Ted had asked her when they stopped for lunch and she chose to eat alone.

"It's nothing, just feeling under the weather and didn't want to bring you guys down too," she had lied.

Lies. They were at the foundation of this entire enterprise.

The radio crackled to life, distracting her from her negative musings, and Beth's voice called out to her.

"I'm struggling in this rain, Kat. Are we stopping soon? It's pretty scary."

"Don't worry, it's not much further. Stay calm and hold on tightly to the tiller. We're about twenty minutes away and then we'll all need to help fasten the boats tightly to the bank. This storm is set to get worse tonight."

Beth acknowledged and the radio was silent once more. The rain hammered down and made visibility difficult.

Although Kat wore a waterproof jacket and trousers, she felt the cold in her bones. Usually, the rain didn't bother her, but tonight it fuelled her mood. She knew, however, that she had to keep it together until they were safely moored. Jordan might have been an asshole, again, but his and all the crew's safety still fell on her shoulders.

Beth did a good job of lining up *Dreamcatcher* with the bank behind the *Creaky Cauldron* in the driving rain. They moored the boats as close together as they could, and Kat set about securing the ropes to the mooring pins.

"Make sure it's tight," she yelled across to Cole, who was pulling *Dreamcatcher* as flush with the bank as he could. "We don't want you coming loose and drifting off in the middle of the night."

Dark storm clouds filled the sky as a blanket of sheet lightning flashed like someone had flicked a switch, and then it was gone. Thunder cracked and rumbled above them.

The unease on Cole's furrowed brow tugged at her.

"It's going to be okay; I promise," she said, smiling to try to reassure him.

"If you say so."

Beth was trying to film them as they tied up the boats, but the rain and wind screamed around them, making any decent footage almost impossible.

"Anyone watching this won't be able to see a thing," she shouted above the roar of the winds.

"Don't worry, I've set up a camera above the door to capture the outside of the boat," Cole said, pointing at the tiny new addition to the *Creaky Cauldron*. "Ted wanted to get some weather shots as he thought it might add a bit of tension to the series."

"Well, there's plenty of tension with this lot," Beth shouted as the thunder cracked above them once again.

"Maybe they'll think they've tuned in to *The Perfect Storm*," Kat offered with a laugh, trying to relieve the crew's anxiety.

As Beth fiddled with her phone and tried to wipe the raindrops from the viewfinder, her foot gave way on the muddy towpath and she pitched forward towards the canal.

Cole's reaction was instant as he grabbed the back of her coat and pulled her to safety, nestling her in his arms.

"Holy shit!" she squealed. "Thank you."

Kat watched Beth bury her face into Cole's chest. Her shoulders began to wobble as the adrenaline faded and the shock of a near miss hit her. Her gentle sobs were drowned out by the thunder.

"I don't like this at all," Beth said, wiping the tears from her face. "Can we all stay together tonight?"

Kat had hoped the crew would all sleep together on *Dreamcatcher* so she could have the *Creaky Cauldron* to herself. She was used to stormy nights and quite liked snuggling under her quilt with the sound of rain pounding on the roof and the winds rocking the boat; however, the look of terror on Beth's face was enough to persuade Kat to give in and suggest they all bunk together.

"Why don't we all have dinner together, and then let's see if these winds settle?" Kat knew it was a flimsy statement at best, as the forecast was brutal until the early hours of the morning, but she had to hope she could avoid spending too much time in Jordan's company. She didn't want Ted, Beth, or Cole guessing at what had unfolded because she couldn't hold in her animosity.

"Take her inside," she said to Cole, motioning towards the boat. "She needs a strong coffee and to get out of her wet clothes."

They disappeared inside and Kat returned her attention to the ropes. Cole's quick reflexes had saved Beth from pitching into the freezing canal water. Wasn't that what love was all about? She shook her head again as the lightning lit up the sky above her. Love. That had never been on the cards for her and Jordan. Who was she kidding? In truth, she should have expected a one-night stand and nothing more, and that realisation hit her hard in the gut. On reflection, she had been as hungry for him as he was for her and hadn't stopped to think about the repercussions.

No sooner had she thought about Jordan than he appeared at her side, his heavy jacket zipped up to his neck and the hood covering most of his face. He knelt down next to her and grabbed the rope she was holding, brushing his fingers against hers.

"Show me what you need me to do," he said, lifting his face and looking directly at her. Her stomach flipped at his touch, and as the rain glistened off his features, she was momentarily reminded of Neptune, god of the sea.

"It's done," she snapped, standing abruptly so she could make a quick getaway.

Jordan stood in her path and reached for her arms, bracing them by her sides and halting her movements. Her mind flashed back to the night his hands had caressed her arms, but she shook her head to dislodge the memory.

"I'm sorry," Jordan said. "The last thing I wanted to do was hurt you, and yet that's exactly what I've ended up doing. How many times do you need me to apologise?"

"You've got nothing to apologise for. We were both unprofessional, so let's forget it ever happened and move on." She wriggled free of his grasp and stormed off to secure the stern, the thunder clapping along with the beat of her footsteps. He sounded sincere with his apologies, but she couldn't shake the doubts that bubbled up inside her. Every time she lowered her guard and let a man in, she ended up getting hurt. Jordan knew how much damage Paul had done to her heart and how broken she felt, but he had swooped in and taken advantage. More importantly, she had let him. Although she was filled with shame, and anger for Jordan and all the other men who had let her down, she was also furious with herself.

With both boats secured, she instructed everyone who wasn't already sheltering from the weather to get inside. Ted was cooking the evening meal, and the smell that met her as she entered the *Creaky Cauldron* made her mouth water.

"If you all leave your dirty boots and wet coats in the bathroom for now," she directed as she began peeling off her soaking garments. "There are towels on my bed if you need one."

As Ted pottered in the kitchen, humming to himself while he stirred and chopped, the rest of them relaxed in the living space. Kat offered her favourite chair to Martha, who had returned from the States just before the weather broke. She gratefully sank into the seat, exhausted from her trip. Cole, Beth, and Jordan squeezed onto the sofa, which left Kat curling up on the floor with a blanket over her legs and her back against the bookshelf.

"How do you cope in the storms when you're alone, Kat?" Martha asked. She looked like she hadn't slept in weeks, and Kat worried that she had pushed herself too far with two long-haul flights in quick succession. Nobody spoke about her whirlwind trip back to LA. Kat wondered if that was a work thing, as in, they didn't discuss home life while on assignment, or whether Martha had chosen not to open up about the visit. Judging by the rings around her eyes, Kat assumed it hadn't been a pleasant trip.

"I'm used to all weathers," she responded, trying to lighten her voice to calm Martha and Beth, who she knew were freaked out by the wind and rain. "The snow and ice are more trouble than a rainstorm, but I make sure I'm back at Mapleton Marina for the winter so I can stay put and be close to my friends."

"Don't you ever wish you had a house on dry land?" Beth asked as she finished towel drying her long hair. "Close to a hairdresser."

Kat laughed at her expression. "And here I was thinking you were having fun."

Beth's face shifted as if she'd realised how negative her question sounded. "I didn't mean anything by it, Kat. I've had a blast on this trip, and you know it."

Kat didn't miss Cole threading his fingers into Beth's and squeezing her hand. They had both had a lot of fun, but they had also found something more.

"I'm only teasing," Kat said with a smile. "I know you're having fun, and I've loved every second of showing you my home and favourite bars and restaurants."

"What's been your favourite part of this trip?" Jordan asked, his gaze flicking from her eyes to her lips.

Kat felt the heat creep up her cheeks. She was overly aware of Cole and Beth staring at her, waiting for an answer, and Martha digging through the oversized handbag in her lap, but all she could think of was Jordan's hands on her body and his lips on hers.

"I reckon it's going to be Ted's dinner," she said, raising her voice so the chef could hear her. His appreciative wave made them all laugh. Crisis averted.

"Oh no, I've left my notebook in *Dreamcatcher*," Martha said, dramatically snapping her handbag shut. "Kat, will you come with me to get it?" She uncurled herself from the seat.

Back in the waterproofs and linking arms like they were about to tackle Mount Everest, they slowly made their way back to the other boat, which bobbed up and down as the wind stirred up the water.

The hedgerows that edged the towpath lit up as lightning flashed across the sky once more, and the big oak trees danced in a frenzy as the wind lifted their branches and shook them violently.

They hurried inside, and Martha quickly found her notebook. However, instead of sliding it into her coat and leaving, she shed her coat and sat down at the table.

"I think we need to talk," she said, patting the seat beside her.

Kat's mouth went dry as she took off her coat and slid into the bench seat next to Martha. Had Jordan told her about their torrid one-night stand? Was this where Martha demanded a refund for fraternising with the star?

"I leave for a few days and everything goes to shit," she said calmly. "I thought you and Jordan were starting to get along. What happened?"

One of the qualities she liked the most about Martha was her directness and no-nonsense approach to life, but right now, she wished she wasn't in the line of fire.

"We're getting along fine," she said, the lie getting lodged in her throat as she spoke.

"Bullshit! What's happened? And I want the truth."

There was no getting away from it. She needed to confess. If it meant the end of Floating Solo, then so be it, but it was killing her to keep her emotions bottled up. Stephanie could only support her so much from afar, and Kat was conscious that her friend was now pregnant and didn't need external drama in her life.

"I slept with Jordan." As she said the words, she was glad it was out in the open. Jordan's desire to keep it to themselves made it seem like a dirty little secret.

"I'm going to assume this was mutually consensual, and neither of you were under the influence of alcohol."

Martha's response took Kat aback, but then it dawned on her that Jordan's string of relationships meant she, as his agent, must have had a million conversations like this one. All of a sudden, she was back to feeling like the dirty little secret.

Hanging her head like the school headmaster was

telling her off, Kat mumbled her confirmation. "It wasn't planned," she said, as if that explained everything. "He was different, and we were bonding, but then one thing led to another."

"I love that boy, so help me God, but he drives me crazy. I've cleaned up so many of his relationship messes over the years, and I'm tired of it. I thought Lexi Chivers might finish me off, but you. You might be the one that breaks me."

Kat's eyes filled with tears at Martha's words, and nothing could stop them from spilling down her face. Instead of the anger she expected, Martha leaned forward and held Kat's face in her hands. Her smile was warm as she brushed the tears away with her thumbs.

"I thought you might be the one to help him find his way. I wanted you to be his guiding light. I didn't want you to be like all the rest. You deserve so much more."

Kat understood now. Martha hoped that Kat's quiet, calm, and safe little life might be the medicine her Hollywood star needed to cure him of all his wicked ways; instead, she had walked the same path as everyone else and given in to the temptation.

"I didn't set out to disappoint you," she whispered. "He got under my skin."

"I know. He has a way of making you love and hate him in equal measure, doesn't he? No matter, I'll speak to him."

"No. Please don't say anything. He's apologised for being unprofessional and taking advantage, and we've agreed to never talk about it again."

"He apologised?"

"Yes, the next day, he went out and bought us coffee, and then he launched into a pitiful apology about how bad he felt and that he shouldn't have crossed that line, and he's kept apologising ever since."

Martha released her hands from Kat's face and smiled. "Maybe there's still hope."

"I don't understand."

"When I say I have to clean up his messes, it means *I'm* the one doing the apologising and offering platitudes and excuses on his behalf. Part of me worried that you would kick us all off the boats before we made it back."

Kat laughed, flopping back in the chair. "I would never do that. In fact, I was the one who thought you would be mad at me. In all honesty, Jordan's right. We shouldn't have slept together, but we did, and we're adults who should be able to talk it through without acting like petulant children."

The disappointment was still there, but Kat felt the anger release as she realised it was her actions that were making the situation uncomfortable. Jordan had apologised repeatedly for his part in this, and it was she who was still holding all the resentment close. From what Martha was saying, this didn't happen often, if at all, so she needed to accept that despite his harsh words, they had come from a good place.

"Let's get back to the others," Martha said, squeezing Kat's arm. "Ted's a great cook, so we're in for a treat."

They locked the door of *Dreamcatcher* and battled through the rain towards the *Creaky Cauldron*. In the blackness, Kat could see Beth on the well deck and Jordan kneeling on the towpath pulling on the rope.

"What happened?" she shouted over the wind.

"Part of the bank gave way, and the mooring pin came loose. The boat started to drift," Jordan yelled back, straining to pull the boat back against the bank.

Kat helped, motioning for Martha to get on board. Beth helped her hop onto the deck before swinging her camera back so she was capturing their ongoing adventures as Kat and Jordan worked together to pull the *Creaky Cauldron* back to the bank again.

Once the rope was tied off again and the mooring pin more secure, they climbed back on board. Jordan made his way towards the door as Kat checked the buoys she had hung around the edge of the bow. If any of the ropes came loose, she wanted to know that they had a cushion against any other boats or the other side of the riverbank.

The thunder cracked above them as the lightning lit up the night sky. Above the boat, a giant oak tree groaned against the strength of the wind. A crack filled the air as one of the older branches broke off under the strain.

Kat couldn't move out of the way in time and took the full force of the bough as it struck her on the head, knocking her backwards. She could hear Beth and Martha shout over the sound of the thunder. The pain in her head was unbearable. As she swiped at her face to clear the blood and rain out of her eyes, she stumbled to the side and pitched overboard, hitting the water as everything went black.

Chapter Fourteen

The soft beep beep beep of a machine lulled Kat from her strange dreams of Neptune and Treebeard of Fangorn Forest, and she let her eyes flicker open. Her head ached, but not in a 'one bottle of wine too many' kind of way. The memories of the storm and being knocked into the canal came flooding back, and she lifted her hand to touch her head. Someone had secured a bandage around her forehead and she winced when touching the wound.

"Omigod, you're awake!" Stephanie's voice pierced the silence and made Kat jump. "Kat, Kat, can you hear me?"

Her friend's face loomed into view and she blinked to focus.

"Hey, what are you doing here?"

"What am I doing here? I'll tell you what I'm doing here. I'm freaking out because my best friend got knocked out by a falling tree and nearly drowned."

"I think you're being a bit dramatic," Kat said, trying to sit up but being restricted by Stephanie's hands against her shoulders.

"Don't even think about trying to get out of this bed until the doctor has been to check on you. What the hell were you doing out in that storm?"

"I wasn't out in it. The boat came loose and we were tying it back up, and I wanted to check the buoys. It was a freak accident, that's all."

"Freak accident. My god, Kat, I never want to receive a call like that again, do you hear me."

"What call?"

Kat wasn't sure which way was up. The accident felt like it had only just happened, but if Stephanie was there, it had to have been some time ago to allow her friend the time to travel to the hospital.

"Beth called me in hysterics, screaming down the phone that you were at the bottom of the canal and Jordan had jumped in after you but couldn't find you in the dark, and…"

"Wait, Jordan jumped in after me?"

A warm glow spread up Kat's spine at the thought of Jordan saving her life. She had watched him save a million girls in his movies, but to know he had done that in real life made her stomach flip.

"Yes, Jordan jumped in after you. He's frantic too, Beth hasn't stopped crying, Martha is a mess, and Ted has been trying to stop the paparazzi from storming the ward to get a look at you."

Kat's eyes grew wide, and Stephanie couldn't help but laugh.

"Yes, the paparazzi are camped outside the hospital," she said with a lopsided smile.

"Why?"

"You are so clueless, Kat. The entire world is watching Beth's little live videos of you and Jordan on the canal having the time of your life. They're invested in whatever is going on between you, and then there's a big dramatic storm and Beth livestreams the entire bloody thing."

"She caught the accident?"

"Hell yeah. It's brutal to watch. You really took that branch full force in the face and then over you went. She caught the splash, the screams, and then Jordan hurling himself into the water after you. It's not the best piece of footage she's ever shot, but honestly, it's gone viral."

It felt surreal to think that hundreds of people across the world were watching a simple accident, but if it helped raise the profile for Ted's docuseries, then she was pleased, although she could have done without the throbbing headache.

"Where is everyone else?" Kat asked. Translation – where was Jordan?

"They're in the waiting room with Tom. You've been out of it for hours, so he's been looking after them and grabbing coffee and biscuits. I think Beth might need something a bit stronger though. She's really shaken up, poor thing."

Kat felt bad for putting her through that. She had dealt with a fair few dramas and accidents over her years on the canal, but she had always been on her own without witnesses. From what Stephanie was saying, it was fortunate that they were with her for this particular incident; otherwise, who knew what the outcome could have been.

As the what-ifs hit her, she began shaking uncontrollably and tears tumbled down her face.

"Oh god, Stephanie. What if Jordan hadn't been there or couldn't save me?"

Stephanie perched on the edge of the hospital bed and grabbed Kat's hand as if she had been expecting this reaction.

"I know. We've all gone through the what-ifs waiting for you to wake up. There is no need to dwell on that. You survived. You're a bit battered and bruised, but you're stitched up and here with us. Focus on that."

Kat nodded but stopped, as the action hurt her head. Squeezing her friend's hand, she lay back on the pillow and stared up at the ceiling, trying to focus on the small fact that she was alive and not at the bottom of the canal.

"Is she awake?" Beth's voice cut into Kat's thoughts, and she lifted her head to see the petite blonde poking her head around the green hospital curtain.

"Hi." Kat raised her hand and gave a little wave, which jolted Beth into action. She rushed forward and flung herself across Kat in a tight hug, tears flowing freely down her face.

"I'm so glad you're okay, Kat. I honestly thought that branch had killed you. It was awful, and then Jordan couldn't find you, which made it even worse."

"Couldn't find me?" Kat turned to Stephanie for confirmation.

"You fell awkwardly and struck the side of the boat before hitting the water, which meant you were pitched further out into the canal. With it being so dark and windy, no one could see where you had risen to the surface after the fall."

Kat swallowed and lay her head back against the pillow again.

"You drifted a bit further along the canal in the wind and got snagged in the reeds," Stephanie added.

Kat's muscles tightened as thoughts of her being pulled to the canal bed by bulrushes rolled through her mind.

"Oh, sorry. I didn't mean to scare you, Kat. It was so dark and crazy, and everything happened so fast. When I got to the side of the boat and looked down into the water, you were gone. I guess I assumed you went straight down." Beth wiped at her eyes and gave Kat a sheepish smile.

"It's okay, Beth. I'm here, and everything turned out for the best."

One by one, the others popped in to see her: first, Martha, with tight hugs and lots of fussing and tweaking the cushion behind Kat's head, and then Ted, who kept telling her he had saved the dinner he had cooked to celebrate her return to the *Creaky Cauldron*.

Cole dropped a bar of chocolate on the nightstand and promised not to film her until her stitches came out, which made her laugh out loud and then wince at the pain.

"Is Jordan okay?" she finally asked when he was the only one who had yet to visit her bedside.

Martha patted her hand. "He's in with the doctor now."

"The doctor? Why? What's wrong?"

"Nothing. We just wanted to get him checked over by a professional. It's usually his stuntmen that do the dangerous things like flinging themselves into a canal, not him."

Martha giggled but Kat didn't miss the tension around

her eyes and the constant flicker of her gaze towards the door.

"He'll be okay," Ted said, probably more for Martha's benefit than Kat's.

As if he knew they were talking about him, Jordan finally stepped around the curtain.

Stephanie shooed everyone out of the room and squeezed Kat's hand before following them outside.

Jordan's face was streaked with mud, and he wore an odd assortment of hospital scrub trousers and what looked like Cole's jacket. His eyes were haunted as he watched everyone file out, leaving them alone.

"Thank you," Kat said as he took a seat in the small plastic chair next to the hospital bed, "for saving my life."

His head hung down so she couldn't see his face, but he nodded slightly to acknowledge he had heard her.

"What you did was brave and stupid." Kat half laughed. "You could have hurt yourself or worse, and Ted would never forgive me if anything happened to you."

She could tell by the slope of his shoulders that he was struggling, whether with emotion or sheer exhaustion from jumping in after her, and she wanted to make him feel better. She wanted to see him smile and hear him laugh. She was alive. He was okay.

"I've never felt pain like that before," he whispered.

Kat reached for his hand and slid her fingers into his.

"That's what happens when you jump into a canal in the middle of a storm. What did the doctor say when they checked you over? Did you need stitches too? You'll probably end up with a horrible cold."

He lifted his head and Kat gasped at the tears in his eyes. "I'm not talking about physical pain, Kat. When that branch hit you and you went over the side, I couldn't move fast enough. The pain in here…" he placed his free hand over his chest "…was unbearable."

She didn't know what to say. Tears spilt over and trailed their way down his handsome face, leaving tracks in the grime.

Kat leaned over and placed her palm on his cheek. "I'm sorry I frightened you," she said softly.

He didn't answer. Instead, he leaned forward and pressed his lips to hers. There was sorrow, relief, and passion in the kiss.

Despite the recent events between them and the shame, frustration, and disappointment Kat felt, she didn't hesitate to slide her fingers into his hair and pull him closer as she kissed him back. The pent-up emotions she had been bottling up broke free as she gave in to a tsunami of joy and desire. She had let him get under her skin, whether that was right or wrong, and in that moment, she firmly believed that kissing Jordan Harrington should be available on prescription.

Breaking away, Jordan sat back in the chair and let out a deep sigh. She couldn't work out if it was a sigh of relief or regret.

"Everything okay?"

"I keep seeing it all unfold in my head," he said, vigorously rubbing his face. "The tree branch, you disappearing over the side, how black the water was, and finally seeing you face down in the reeds."

She reached for his hand and squeezed his fingers. "I'm right here, and we're both alright. There's nothing to worry about."

"But what if I hadn't…?"

"Don't do that, Jordan. Please. You saved my life and we're both going to be fine."

Jordan smiled across at her, although his brow stayed furrowed, and all she wanted to do was smooth his worries away.

He stayed by her side for a while, neither of them speaking as the nurses came in to check on her routinely. They sat in silence with fingers entwined, enjoying the stillness of the early hours. Eventually, Ted tugged Jordan from the bedside with instructions to leave Kat to sleep and to get back to the boat for a warm shower and clean clothes.

"I'll be back in the morning," he said, kissing her one last time.

Stephanie had dropped off an overnight bag with some underwear, clothes, toiletries, and Kat's phone, which the nurse left with her before instructing her to get some sleep.

Even though she was shattered, and her bruised body longed for rest, she couldn't switch off her brain. Thoughts of the accident steamrolled their way through her mind until she couldn't think about anything else. She needed to see it for herself. Pulling her phone from the bag, she searched for Beth's Instagram feed and found the video. It had been viewed over five million times, and the comments section contained thousands of messages sending love and support to the crew.

'*Thinking of you all.*'

'*Stay safe and look after each other.*'

'*Jordan is a real-life hero.*'

'*Sending our love.*'

It was heartwarming to read the messages from people she had never met but who were so invested in this adventure. As she scrolled through them all, she spotted a familiar name. Paul's comment stood out, as it was so typically him, short and to the point, and it made her chuckle in the quiet hospital ward.

'*Kathryn never let anything defeat her. All the best, Paul.*'

He was right, of course. Everything that life had thrown at her, she had dealt with, overcome, or allowed to make her stronger, and this situation was no different, although it troubled her that his message read like an obituary.

Pushing aside the clear fact that she seemed to be dead to Paul, she hoped the storm wouldn't deter prospective travellers from experiencing her Floating Solo experience. She wanted this accident to empower people and help them recognise how fragile life could be and embrace every adventure.

As she scrolled back up the page, she reached the video and tentatively hovered her finger over the play icon. After turning down the volume so it didn't wake the other patients, she started the video.

Beth's shaky hand struggled to keep still as the rain soaked her. Big droplets of water clung to the camera's lens before running down the screen. Kat could see Jordan on the towpath pulling the boat closer to the bank as she and Martha arrived. The camera jostled as Beth helped Martha to climb on board, mumbling about getting inside to the warmth of the *Creaky Cauldron*. Beth stayed close to the door, panning her phone camera around to capture Kat and Jordan securing the boat as she gave a running commentary of what was happening, her voice getting drowned out every once in a while by the booming thunder.

The phone jolted again as Jordan boarded and stood beside Beth with one hand on the door handle. Kat watched herself jump onto the well deck and move to the right side to check the buoys as Beth zoomed in on the roiling canal and the flash of lightning. In the blinding light, Kat was illuminated against the backdrop of trees bending and shaking in the distance, with the wind whistling through the phone's microphone. The footage was raw and scary. Anyone watching would have thought they were crazy standing out in that weather, but then Kat heard the crack. The memory of hearing it the first time hit her hard as the footage continued on her screen.

The branch smashed into Kat's head, knocking her backwards. The phone shook violently as Beth shouted out. Kat watched herself flounder and stumble, trying to wipe the blood and rain out of her eyes before falling overboard at an odd angle. For her, that was where the memory ended. Everything went black as she hit the water, but for those left on the boat, the horror kept unfolding.

Beth's shouts mingled with Martha's scream and the roar of the wind, and then Jordan flashed past the screen, leaning over the boat and shouting at the water.

The camera pitched and rolled as Beth clung to her phone but moved around the deck.

"I can't see her!" Jordan yelled back at Beth.

The door of the *Creaky Cauldron* opened, splashing warm lamplight over the well deck as the others dashed outside, roused by the commotion.

Kat watched as Jordan launched himself overboard and splashed into the canal. Beth's hand never stopped shaking as her voice filled the air.

"What's he doing? Oh god, get them out, get them out."

Beth moved forward, and for a short while, the film showed the back of Cole and Ted's heads as they hung over the side, trying to help Jordan.

Over the wind, Kat could hear his frantic shouts from the water.

"She's not here! I can't find her."

Then Cole yelled something inaudible and pointed behind the boat, out of the camera's view. Jordan swam out of sight, and Kat sucked in her breath. Even though she knew what had happened, the entire film was captivating.

The footage was raw, nothing like the fun and seamless behind-the-scenes videos Beth had previously shared. Kat wasn't even sure that Beth remembered she was still livestreaming, as most of the shots were of the deck and the water. There was an urgency to the video fuelled by the panicked shouts of the crew and the way the camera shook. It momentarily reminded Kat of *The Blair Witch Project* she and her friends had sneakily watched at a sleepover when they were youngsters and terrified themselves silly.

When Jordan finally reappeared in the shot, he was dragging an unconscious Kat along with him. She gasped as she watched the footage of herself covered in blood.

Lifting her hand from the phone, she touched the bandage on her head again. In the video, all you could see was blood pouring from the deep gash on her head. Her eyes were closed and her body was limp. Jordan pulled her along, shouting instructions to Ted and Cole as between them they lifted her out of the water and onto the deck.

Jordan hoisted himself over the edge with Cole's help and dropped to his knees beside her, feeling for a pulse and starting CPR, and then the film cut out.

She stared at the 'play again' message on her screen for what felt like an eternity. No wonder everyone was so freaked out, and no wonder there were so many messages. Without knowing what happened next, it looked like Kathryn Sinclair's dead body had just been pulled from the deep.

Chapter Fifteen

"It doesn't take all of you to manhandle me out of a wheelchair." Kat sighed as five sets of hands reached forward to steady her.

The hospital had discharged her, and the entire crew had descended to pick her up and bring her back to where the *Creaky Cauldron* was moored.

She stood by the open door of one of Martha's hired Range Rovers and smiled at her assembled friends.

"I'm fine, I promise. It's my head that took the bashing, not my legs."

A porter claimed the now vacant wheelchair and scurried away, dodging the crowd of reporters who were snapping photographs and searching for a newsworthy scoop.

Ted sauntered over to them, leaving Kat to slide into the back of the car as they pounced eagerly on the director with a barrage of questions.

How is she? Any permanent damage? Are they in a relationship? Has filming stopped? What does this mean for your docuseries?

"We're happy to report that Miss Sinclair is in full health. She sustained a small head injury and had to have seven stitches, but she's a tough cookie and is eager to get back to the canal and our filming schedule."

Was Jordan hurt? How is he?

"Mr Harrington is in good spirits. He was unharmed during the accident, and we are all grateful he was there to save Miss Sinclair's life. His heroic actions and Miss Sinclair's drive and professionalism are why we are able to keep filming."

He left it there and sauntered back to the waiting cars as they called after him wanting more. The flash of the cameras made Kat blink and cover her eyes with her hand. How did Jordan deal with this every single day?

"How do you feel?" Jordan sat beside her in the back of the car and took her hand in his as the cars drove away from the hospital.

"A bit gobsmacked if I'm honest. I would expect the press to camp outside a hospital for you but not for me."

He laughed, and it lit up his face. Kat had only seen the deep grooves on his forehead as he fussed over her the last twenty-four hours, and it was a pleasant change to see his smile.

"You're a star too now," he said, winking at her. "Kathryn Sinclair, headline act in Carry On Boating, or should that be *floating*."

Kat burst out laughing. "How do you know about the Carry On films? I thought they were quintessentially British."

"Are you kidding? Ted's a huge fan and used to force me to watch them so I could understand your British humour. He thought it would make me more universally popular."

"Well, if Ted decides to turn this docuseries into the next Carry On film, I'm totally in. My dad would be so proud, as they were his favourite."

They sat in silence as the car swept through the streets, heading for the boats, Jordan's fingers still entwined in Kat's. It felt comfortable to be sitting together holding hands, and yet she knew it could only be down to Jordan's fear and the adrenaline of recent events.

Nothing had changed. Yes, they'd kissed in the hospital, but she knew he needed that, probably more than she did. Jordan and the rest of them were still heading home in a few days.

When they walked down to the boats, there was a small gathering on the towpath. Stephanie, Tom, and Roger were waiting for them with a sign saying, 'Welcome home' and a batch of homemade cookies, and a few other fans and locals had braved the muddy pathways to see them return.

The storm had blown through eventually, leaving localised flooding and felled trees across the county, and the large oak that towered over the *Creaky Cauldron* was silent as they approached, its dance of destruction over. Bits of branches, twigs, and leaves littered the bow and stern of the *Creaky Cauldron*. Kat's herb pots had been scattered, with some broken and spilling soil onto the roof. She walked along the towpath, giving the boat a quick once-over. There was minimal damage, for which she was grateful, and nothing that couldn't be cleaned up in a few hours.

Although the skies were still grey, the sun was trying to force its way through to add some warmth and joy to the proceedings.

"Oh, Kat, we were so worried about you." Roger pulled her in for a tight hug, and she rested her head on his chest, thankful for a reminder of home. It wouldn't be long until they were back at Mapleton Marina. She felt like she had been away for months.

"It's good to see you," she said. "Have you closed the shop to be here?" Kat couldn't believe that Roger would do such a thing, but so many strange things had happened recently.

"Goodness me, no. I've left Dotty and Barbara in charge." The strangled expression on his face made her giggle.

"Well, I'm so glad you came, even though I know you're itching to get back and see what mischief they've got up to."

Roger groaned and released his hug to let Tom take his turn.

"Welcome back, Kat."

Stephanie nudged him out of the way so she could have a hug too.

"You guys won't be able to fight over me once that baby comes, you know. The baby will win, hands down," Kat teased.

The three of them huddled together, catching up and talking about the storm as Jordan signed autographs and posed for selfies with the diehard fans who ventured down to the boats, happy to have been a small part of this story. As the small group of admirers left, they called back to Kat.

"Glad you're okay, Kat."

"Great to have you back, Kat."

She smiled and waved at them as they walked away. Jordan joined her and slipped his arm around her shoulder.

She didn't miss the look Stephanie and Tom exchanged.

"Ted thinks it might be best to stay put for another night and set off tomorrow rather than rushing into anything. Is that okay with you?" Jordan asked.

An extra day with Jordan?

"Yes, that sounds great," Kat said.

He said his goodbyes to Stephanie, Tom, and Roger and wandered back to *Dreamcatcher* to check on Martha.

"What's going on with you two?" Stephanie asked, pulling Kat to the side and being the only one of her friends to get straight to the point.

"Nothing. He kissed me in the hospital, but I honestly think he was still running on adrenaline. It meant nothing." The words stuck in her throat as she said them.

To her, his kiss meant everything, as did his smile, his touch, his scent, and being in his presence.

"You're going to get your heart broken again if you're not careful," Stephanie said softly. "You do remember what Paul did. Only a matter of days ago, might I add."

"I know I hit my head, but I don't have brain damage. Of course I remember what Paul did. I remember what *everyone* has done to me over the years, but this isn't like that. We had a moment, it was epic, but it's over, and that's that."

Stephanie gave her the look she used when she knew she was being lied to. "I'm sorry, Kat, but I know you better than you know yourself, and no amount of deflecting can hide the fact that you are falling for Jordan Harrington."

"It's under control," Kat added, somewhat unconvincingly.

"We'll see," Stephanie mumbled. "In the meantime, I've managed to fend off Paul, as he wanted to see you. Despite being a total wanker, I think he was genuinely worried about you."

"I don't believe that for a second. His comment on Beth's video was about as warm as the canal water."

"Yeah, I saw it and I pulled him up on it too, but he seemed a bit cut up about you two leaving things on such bad terms. I know he's an idiot, but you guys do have history. It's only right he shows some emotion over your accident."

It gave Kat a moment of peace to know he still cared about her. Yes, he had done a terrible thing, but Stephanie was right. They had shared three years together, and that was hard to let go of.

"I'm glad he knows I'm okay, but I don't want to see him – ever."

"Leave it to me."

Kat knew Stephanie and Tom had her back, and she said a silent farewell to her old life, knowing Paul would never be a part of it again.

She waved Stephanie, Tom, and Roger off when they left her a while later, Stephanie's warning about Jordan still ringing in Kat's ears. Everything her friend told her was right. There was no future in giving in to fantasy, but just for one day, she wanted to languish in that make-believe world.

★ ★ ★

Everyone agreed that Kat should rest in her bed until dinnertime, leaving Ted to get started on his second attempt at cooking them all dinner.

Martha nudged open the door to Kat's bedroom and handed her a steaming mug of coffee before taking a seat on the edge of the bed.

"I mentioned there was something I wanted to talk to you about," she said, playing with the hem of her blouse. "Before I had to go see my uncle."

Kat remembered that conversation, but with all the excitement, she had pushed it from her mind.

"You told me about Paul and how he let you down on the investment side of your business. Well, I would like to invest instead."

Kat stopped the cup midway to taking a sip and stared over the rim at Martha to see if she was teasing her. The big brown eyes that stared back were full of warmth and expectation.

"Are you serious?"

"I am. I knew the moment I met you that I wanted to do something to help, but I wasn't sure what that was back then. The more I got to know you and this beautiful boat, the more determined I was. Then I went back to LA and was with my uncle as he died…"

Kat gasped. "Why didn't you tell us?" She had sensed that Martha was distracted when she returned but had assumed it was jetlag or more Jordan drama.

"It's a private matter, and I didn't want my grief to affect everyone's work. Besides, before he passed, he told me I needed to live a little and be more adventurous." She smiled at the memory. "He was larger than life, loved to travel, and could never understand why I was so invested in other people's work."

"I guess being an agent is all about other people, so I understand why he would want you to do something for yourself," Kat said. "Your uncle sounds like my dad. He always wanted the best for me."

"I believe in you, Kat. Seeing what you are doing here has made me happy. I told my uncle about you when I saw him and that I wanted to help but didn't know how. It was his idea to invest in your business. He would have loved the *Creaky Cauldron*."

Martha looked around Kat's bedroom, taking in the creamy yellow walls, the blue and grey fabric bunting that hung down from the ceiling, and the ornaments that added that homely feel to each room.

"It's been a joy sharing your home with you, and I want to continue being a part of your life when this trip ends."

"Are you staying in England?" Kat asked.

"Goodness me, no, my home is in LA, but I'm confident that you would be able to handle a silent partner who only pops in once or twice a year for a solo holiday." Martha's smile was wide and her eyes sparkled. "So, what do you think?"

Kat placed the coffee cup on the nightstand and pulled Martha into a warm hug. She clung to her like a child to a mother. "Thank you, Martha. I don't know what to say."

"Say nothing, not yet. Let's complete this docuseries before we tell the rest of them the news. Otherwise, they'll think they can stay with you forever and never go back home."

Kat didn't think that was such a bad thing, even though Martha laughed at her own words. Her business was going to expand after all, and if Martha was her silent partner *and* Jordan's agent, then there was a strong possibility that they would remain in each other's lives one way or another, which made Kat's heart skip a beat.

"We've got time to work out the details and draw up contracts. In the meantime, I want us to enjoy the last few days of this trip and make sure you are fully fit."

"Don't worry about me," Kat said, squeezing her new partner's hand. "You've just given me the best reason to keep fighting for my dreams."

Martha leaned in. "I think my uncle would be proud of both of us."

Kat smiled at her, recognising the sadness in her eyes. When she lost her dad, it changed her entire life, but she always felt his presence. Perhaps her dad and Martha's uncle would be watching over them together.

Ted interrupted their bonding by announcing that dinner was served, and Kat was glad for an excuse to get out of bed and move around. She hated feeling like an invalid.

"We need to give the public what they want." Beth said after everyone had cleared their plates and moved to the living space to relax. This time, Kat received her favourite chair, while Beth and Martha snuggled on the sofa and the boys scattered around the floor.

"And what do the public want?" Ted asked, draining his glass of wine.

"They want to know that Kat is okay. The last behind-the-scenes video I shared was from the storm. If people haven't seen the news, then they might assume Kat is, well, you know…"

"Dead!" Kat finished for her. "I think Beth's right. We need to do a follow-up."

Everyone looked at Kat and she burst out laughing at their expressions. "I'm not saying I enjoy this being on film malarky, but I am happy to confirm that I'm alive and kicking. There might be old boyfriends out there sobbing over my faded school photographs thinking I'm gone."

Beth threw a cushion at Kat as the crew laughed in unison.

"Stop making fun of me; I'm serious. There are a lot of comments from people asking what happened and if we're all okay."

"She's right," Jordan said. "It would be easy to film us all here enjoying a night of good food and conversation. We could even play a game."

"As long as it's not strip poker then I'm up for that," Kat said.

She saw Jordan wince and wished she could take that back. The half-naked women in her living room felt like forever ago, and he had more than apologised for his indiscretions.

"How about a good old-fashioned game of charades?" Martha suggested.

They divided into teams, all vying for the coveted title of Floating Solo champion.

At Ted's request, the game had to have a film twist, with Martha easily recognising his attempt at *Jaws* and taking them into an early lead.

"We've got this." Jordan winked at Kat as it got to their turn. He rubbed his hands down his jeans as if preparing for an arm-wrestling competition instead of charades.

Stomping around the small interior of the *Creaky Cauldron*, Jordan held his arms tight to his body and hooked his hands into claws.

"*Fight Club*," Kat yelled.

He shook his head and continued stomping back and forth. His expression could have been mistaken for indigestion, and it made Beth snort with laughter.

"*Monsters Inc.*" Kat tried again.

"Seriously. Is my acting *that* bad?" Jordan paused with his hands on his hips.

"YES!" five voices shouted at once.

The laughter bounced off the walls and circled Kat like a warm embrace. She looked at the happy faces of Jordan and his crew giggling, joking around, and enjoying themselves, and a wave of contentment washed over her.

"Come on, Kat, don't let me down now." Jordan picked up where he left off, scratching at the air with his clawed fingers and contorting his face into what looked like a growl.

"*Jurassic Park*," she screamed.

"Yes. Spot on." They high-fived as he slid down onto the floor at her feet, his body touching her legs, distracting her for a moment from their win.

"We make a great team," he said softly as Cole jumped to his feet beside them, ready for his turn with Beth.

The game went on long into the night, switching from films to books. Martha and Ted were the clear winners, but Kat and Jordan came a close second.

Beth captured a lot of the fun on camera, and as Kat watched it back from the sanctuary of her bedroom once everyone had retired for the night, she couldn't help but smile at the scenes. They looked like a family. Watching Jordan act out a book title he had never heard of had them all roaring with laughter, but the highlight was when Kat guessed the right answer and he picked her up to swing her around in celebration.

The comments under the new video were full of warm wishes and happiness that the two were reunited. Beth had been right. Everyone wanted to know what happened next.

So did Kat.

Chapter Sixteen

They had one full day left and an overnight stay, and then the Floating Solo experience would come to an end at Mapleton Marina. The trip had already been extended by two days due to Kat's hospital stay, but now the finish line was in sight.

As Jordan cleaned the bathroom in a pair of bright yellow rubber gloves, Kat stood over him and took a photo.

"That's going on my selfie wall." She chuckled. "Who would have thought I'd have a Hollywood superstar scrubbing my shower cubicle?"

"You're not funny." He laughed. "I reckon I've been the best guest you've ever had on this boat. Go on, admit it."

He waved the Scrub Daddy in her face, making her squeal and run back into the kitchen. She looked at the selfie wall and smiled at all the wonderful pictures and memories they conjured, but she knew without a doubt that Jordan's photo would be the one she would stare at the most in the months and years to come. He had been the most challenging guest, but yes, he was right; he had been the best.

"You've barely any room on this board to add more photos." Jordan hovered over her shoulder as she studied the pictures.

"I'll get a bigger board," she said, giggling.

"After this trip and all the bookings you'll have, I reckon you'll need to use all the walls instead."

She liked the idea of more bookings and boats, but she had promised Martha that she wouldn't mention her investment.

"This girl wrote a book after spending a week with me." Kat pointed at the freelance journalist whose article about her trip had appeared in the newspapers. "And this one has since got married and had a baby. That one moved to the seaside, and this beautiful lady bought a narrowboat of her own up in Hexham, Northumberland. They all keep in touch. Did you know that?"

"I can understand why," he said, his voice soft in her ear. "They would want to keep their memories of this boat and you close."

She half turned, knowing his lips were close enough to kiss, but stopped herself.

"It would be lovely if all of you stayed in touch too."

"Once that photo goes on the board, I reckon it's sealed with a magical spell. You'll never get rid of us."

His words made her pulse quicken. Maybe Martha's decision to become a silent partner would make that magic spell a reality.

★ ★ ★

The last day wasn't about cruising on the canal. They only had a short distance left to travel, so Kat always gave her guests a day off to soak up the late spring/early summer sunshine, enjoy the rest, and take advantage of local shops. Ted had agreed that they all needed a film-free day, giving them all the time to do whatever they wanted. His schedule focused on the grand return to the marina the next day and how that would look.

Beth and Cole had disappeared early to grab some shopping before Ted changed his mind, and Martha had calls and emails to answer, which left Jordan and Kat alone in the *Creaky Cauldron*.

"Cleaning your boat wasn't exactly what I had in mind for my day off, you know," he said, dropping the cleaning products back under the sink in the galley.

"What did you have in mind?" Kat's words came out much breathier than she anticipated, so it sounded flirty, which wasn't her intention. However, the slight rise in Jordan's eyebrow made her wonder if he had been harbouring similar thoughts.

"I thought you could show me around."

Not what she expected, but the idea appealed to her.

"I'd love that. If you've finished all your chores, Cinderella, you can grab your coat and shoes."

He chased her out of the door, laughing as they stumbled onto the footpath. A surprised dog walker tutted as she pulled back on the lead to control her Jack Russell, who was equally startled.

Jordan reached for Kat's hand as they set off down the towpath, and they fell into step beside each other.

There was a cute antique and craft barn close to the main road that ran parallel to the canal, with a selection of small shop units selling everything from bedding plants to wool. It had a café and farm shop on site that sold the most amazing Victoria sponge cake, and that's where Kat decided to take Jordan. She wanted him to experience her world for a while. The one that was full of pleasant chatter, relaxing coffee dates, and beautiful countryside.

On their way along the path and over the bridge towards the craft centre, they passed a few people who did a double-take when spotting Jordan Harrington. She wondered if they knew who he was or if they recognised him but couldn't place where from.

Kat had bumped into a soap actor once and talked to him about the state of the holes in the main roads before walking away and realising he wasn't a local but someone off the telly.

"Martha told me her news," he said as they climbed over the stile leading to the public footpath. "About investing in your business."

She took the hand he offered so she could climb off the step but misjudged her footing and bumped into him. He caught hold of her and lingered before taking a step back to give her room.

"I'm excited that she wants to be part of the business," Kat said, walking away and inviting him to follow. The craft centre was on the other side of the farmer's field. "She has a positive energy about her that matches my own values."

For many years, Kat had tried to fit into friendship groups that didn't work or places of employment that were toxic, and it had taken her a long time to work out what mattered to her the most. Her father had tried to show her what true connection was like without getting sucked in by manipulative people, but the lesson didn't hit home until he died. Suddenly, she was alone and in pain, but her so-called friends kept their distance or walked away. They were only there for what they could get out of her, whether that was physical time or emotional support. In a way, her dad's passing meant she finally understood what he was trying to teach her and she could start over with a clean slate and only surround herself with the right people. The select friends she kept close were those she chose for herself, and her business was so intrinsically linked to her home life that it was vital she get the balance and energy right.

Martha was the perfect fit.

"She had other news too," he said, almost shyly. "Ted has received a couple of scripts that the writers feel would work for me. There's a romantic comedy set in Italy that he's keen on accepting for me as well as a medical drama set in Seattle."

Kat stopped dead in the middle of the field and turned to smile up at him. "That's amazing news, Jordan. I'm so happy for you. I can't believe you kept that to yourself."

"I was a bit nervous, to be honest. Knowing nobody wanted to work with me hit a nerve, and I guess I'm in that zone of 'I'll believe it when I see it' at the moment."

"Ted wouldn't tell you about the scripts if he didn't believe they were genuine. Everything Ted and Martha do is for your benefit."

"I know. My confidence is a bit shaken, that's all."

Kat understood that. Her own confidence had taken a battering recently, so how Jordan felt resonated with her, but she knew deep inside that he was destined for great things.

"Believe in yourself," she said softly. "Like I believe in you."

His lips were on hers before she could register him moving forward. He wrapped his arms around her waist and pulled her tight to him. Her arms snaked around his neck as she lost herself in the kiss. They were panting heavily when they pulled apart, and she scoured the field for anyone who might have caught their passionate embrace, but the countryside was empty.

"I'm sorry, I can't seem to stop kissing you," Jordan said, lifting his fingers to his lips as if sealing the kiss there forever. "I told you I wouldn't take advantage of you again, but…"

"I never thought you did take advantage," she said, finding her voice and bravery despite this being their last day together. "When we slept together, I was the happiest I've been in such a long time, and then you told me it was wrong and unprofessional. That's not how I saw it. It's not how I see it today. I'm sorry that *you* were sorry, but please don't tell me how I feel or what I want, because you have no idea what's in my heart."

Jordan reached forward with his hand and trailed a thumb down her cheek, stopping at her bottom lip and giving her time to kiss the tip of his thumb. His soft smile showed her he wasn't angry at what she had said. In fact, the longing in his eyes told her that his feelings mirrored her own.

"In truth, I only said those things because I thought

I should. Martha has spent years clearing up my messes, and I knew she'd be pissed at me for getting you involved. It wasn't wrong, Kat. I just hated the idea of you thinking less of me, and then I went and messed it all up anyway." He kicked at a lump of grass as he spoke, averting his eyes and looking anywhere but at her. "That night was amazing for me too."

She leaned in and kissed him gently on the cheek before slipping her fingers into his. "Thank you for being honest."

He smiled down at her. "It's the new me."

She chuckled and tugged at his hand and they carried on walking in silence.

Jordan's revelation that their night together meant something to him as well rolled over and over in the back of Kat's mind as she introduced him to the shop owners she had known for years. They welcomed his visit and took lots of photographs, promising to share them on their social media feeds. Jordan was the definition of a celebrity in every way. He attracted admiring glances from everyone and took the time to chat with anyone who stopped them. Not once did he grumble as he posed for selfies and signed the back of till receipts or the clothing people wore. He bought a few gifts for friends back in LA and was the perfect gentleman as they visited every shop. The craft centre buzzed with the high-vibe energy he seemed to leave wherever he went.

Kat found it hard to recall the moody man who stepped out of that Range Rover two weeks earlier as she watched him laughing with a farmer who was sharing a story about a runaway goat. Her mind wandered to that night in the *Creaky Cauldron* and the feel of his hands on her body. She ached for his touch, but despite the kisses and the kind words, she knew their passionate night was nothing more than a one-night stand, and she had to accept that. The next day they would part ways and potentially never see each other again unless Martha brought him along when she came to visit, but that seemed unlikely. He was about to relaunch his career after a turbulent time, and Kat knew nothing could get in the way of that.

Fed, watered, and carrying far too many shopping bags, they made their way back to the canal slowly. The sun was high, and the sky was a clear blue with only a smattering of clouds, in contrast to the storm of a few days ago. Kat felt like the rain had washed away all the bad and made way for a new phase.

"Tell me about your plans once Martha invests," Jordan said as they sauntered back through the fields.

It felt strange for her to talk openly about the dream she had been clinging to for so long. Only Stephanie knew what she wanted to create here, but Jordan's open smile prompted her to share her thoughts.

"The idea is to buy another boat or two and kit them out like the *Creaky Cauldron*. I'd then hire hosts to run the trips. Stephanie suggested we have a boat on every waterway throughout the UK, but that's a big goal for a faraway future."

"It sounds exciting. What you've built here is amazing, Kat. I know I was a grumpy bastard when I first arrived and didn't see the beauty of what you were doing, but I do now.

I get it. Everything works so well, and even the slow pace of life won me over in the end."

She chuckled as she remembered telling her new guests about the four mile per hour speed limit, something they couldn't comprehend, especially when they had come from California.

"Don't get me wrong, I enjoy a lively night out and the bustle of a busy city, but coming back home to the *Creaky Cauldron* always fills me with joy."

"I can see that."

His eyes sparkled as they reached the towpath where the boats were moored together for the final time. Beth was sitting in the sunshine reading a book on the stern of *Dreamcatcher*, and Cole was tinkering with his camera equipment.

"I'll catch up with you later," Jordan said as he hopped onto *Dreamcatcher*. "I need to speak with Ted."

Kat kept walking and jumped on the well deck of the *Creaky Cauldron*; her colourful cushions were out on the bench seats, and the little area looked inviting in the watery sunshine. There was work to do and tasks to complete, but she couldn't muster any enthusiasm to do any of them. There was a hole in her chest, and she felt utterly bereft. The hours were ticking down as the sun began its descent in the sky, inching ever closer to the completion of another Floating Solo experience.

As she walked through the living space, she couldn't help but focus on the tiny details of this trip. She ran her hand along the back of the chair where Martha often sat scribbling in her business notebook, making plans or jotting down her observations. In the kitchen, the pans that Ted used to cook dinner were stacked up on the draining board, following yet another delicious dinner over their fun conversations. She saw the scrap of paper Beth had used to write the scores from their game of charades screwed up on the side table and the small pile of sweet wrappers Cole had discarded when it was his turn to play.

Never before had she been so affected by her guests. Maybe this was how they felt when they told her she had made an impression on them and inspired them to do great things.

She sank down onto the sofa and curled up in a ball, suddenly overcome by tiredness. The doctor had told her she needed to take it easy for a few days, but she didn't think this exhaustion was related to her accident.

Chapter Seventeen

The *Creaky Cauldron* was in darkness when Kat opened her eyes. The sun had set, and night had crept over her without her noticing. She wasn't sure how long she had slept, but panic set in as she grabbed for her phone to check the time. Where was everyone?

She flicked on the lamps and drew the curtains, listening for sounds of life beyond the window. Slipping her shoes on, she hopped off the boat and wandered down to *Dreamcatcher*, hoping to find the crew laughing over their last supper, but the boat was also in darkness. The silence stretched out across the canal.

All the hairs on the back of her neck stood to attention, and she didn't think it was from the breeze coming off the canal.

They had all gone out without her. It was their last night together, and they had left her behind. She felt a tightness in her chest as she looked at *Dreamcatcher*, gently bobbing up and down in the dark. At that exact moment, she felt more alone than she had ever felt before. She couldn't stop the tears that tumbled down her face as she wrapped her arms around herself, feeling foolish. The more she thought about it, the more sense it made. This trip was for them, it was about them as a team, and she was merely the host. It was laughable that she had assumed their connection was real.

As she stumbled back towards the *Creaky Cauldron*, Jordan's voice floated out of the darkness.

"Wait! Kat, where are you going?"

Confusion muddled her brain as she looked around. He hadn't been on the towpath a second ago, and yet there he was, his handsome face crumpled in concern as he saw her tears.

"What's wrong? Are you in pain?"

"I thought I'd lost you," she whimpered.

He wrapped his arms around her and held her tightly as she cried. She wondered if he thought she was crazy or if her bump on the head was more serious than first diagnosed, but he didn't move, he didn't speak, he simply held her while she sobbed. When her tears dried up, and she pushed away from him to wipe at her eyes, she noticed the other faces peering out of *Dreamcatcher*'s doorway.

"Are you coming inside?" Beth shouted.

"Yes, we'll be there in a minute," Jordan answered for them, rubbing his thumb across Kat's cheek to catch a rogue tear.

"You haven't lost me," he said, speaking directly to Kat. "You'll never lose any of us. Come on." He held her hand and tugged her towards *Dreamcatcher*.

Once inside, the lights flipped on and party poppers exploded in the air. A champagne cork popped off to her side as she tried to adjust her bleary eyes to focus on the bunting and the piles of food laid out on the table.

"We wanted to throw you a going-away party," Beth

said excitedly. "The last thing we wanted to do was upset you."

Kat threw herself at the petite blonde and squeezed her so tight she began to squeal.

"I love it. Thank you to all of you. I think the accident has left me feeling a bit more emotional than usual," Kat said, looking at everyone in turn.

Martha's eyes had glassed over too, and she turned abruptly to grab a glass of champagne and swipe at her face.

Ted handed Kat a glass and affectionately kissed her forehead.

"We couldn't leave without showing our amazing host how much we appreciated her and treating her to a final feast, courtesy of Cole and me. We've been busy cooking all afternoon under Jordan's supervision."

Cole took a bow as Beth playfully nudged him out of the way to grab a handful of crisps.

"They've been insufferable," she teased. "It's not hard to open a few packets, guys."

Kat laughed and felt her pulse slow and her shoulders relax. They hadn't abandoned her after all.

"Do you like it?" Jordan tugged her to the side as Beth and Cole duelled with a pair of breadsticks. "When I left you earlier, it was to check if Ted needed help organising everything. I wanted everything to be special for you, but you slept for so long we worried you'd miss your own party. I was on my way to wake you up when I saw you out there."

"I was having a moment," she said. "It was so quiet when I woke up, and I've got used to the chaos that comes with all of you, so it felt strange and unnerving. I was a bit disoriented."

"You'll get your peace and quiet back tomorrow, but we can always leave Beth behind if you think you can't cope with the silence."

"Hey. I heard that." Beth laughed, swatting Jordan on the back of the head.

Kat took her glass of champagne and slid into the bench seat to watch her friends fool around, play fight, talk over one another, and laugh loudly. She didn't think she would ever cope with the silence again. Their vibrant energy had ignited something in her, something she didn't recognise. She had always been so happy and comfortable in her own company, but spending all her time on the water alone had also made her isolated. Perhaps it was time to push herself out into the world. Her business was going to expand with Martha's help, which meant she would have more free time to search for that cottage and grow roots on land.

She was under no illusion that she and Jordan could be anything more than friends, but maybe the entire experience was the reminder she needed that there were good people out there. Not everyone she met was bad news or out to hurt her.

"Hey, y'all, can I have your attention, please?" Ted shouted above the lively conversations. "I think it would be a nice touch to tell our gracious host exactly what we all think of her."

"Oh blimey, I'm not sure I'm up to that," Kat joked.

"Let me go first." Beth shot to her feet and held her champagne flute above her head. "To Kat, thank you for showing us your favourite bars and being my dancing partner, for not throwing my phone in the canal when I forced you to be on my videos, and for being an awesome person."

Glasses clinked and everyone cheered.

"Me next. I want to thank you for slowing me down long enough to see what was right in front of me" Cole took hold of Beth's hand and raised his other, which held a beer bottle. "To our very own cupid."

"Cupid," came the collective cry.

Martha stood up next and held her glass in Kat's direction. "To a beautiful soul who cares deeply about the experiences she offers and the people who share her home. May you have plenty of success in the future."

Kat smiled at the hidden message in Martha's toast. She had told Jordan of her plans to invest, but as yet, no one else knew.

"I agree with Martha," Ted said next, getting to his feet. "When we thought about putting this trip together, and Martha told me about this little Floating Solo business in the middle of the United Kingdom, I'm not gonna lie; I thought she'd lost her mind."

Everyone laughed as Martha threw a bread roll at him.

"But…I was wrong. As usual, Martha knew exactly what we needed to do, and she found us the perfect person to help us achieve it. The buzz this trip has created for all of us is way more than I ever expected, and that's thanks to you, Kat."

He tipped his glass in her direction as everyone yelled, "Kat."

All eyes swung to Jordan, who was sipping his beer but staring at the floor.

"I'm not sure what else I can add that hasn't been said already," he said, lifting his head to look directly at Kat. "You took a spoilt, grumpy actor and turned him into something else."

"You're still grumpy," Cole joked.

Jordan chuckled but didn't let Cole's jibe break his stride. "You've turned this trip into something special for each one of us. Thank you."

Beth handed something to Jordan and bounced up and down like a kid on Christmas morning as he pulled the small box out of the paper bag.

"We got you a little something to remember us by," he said, handing her a white Pandora box. She opened it and gasped. Inside was a silver charm bracelet with three charms attached. The first was a cauldron, which made Kat chuckle. The second was a tiny clapperboard, and the last was a silver coin with 'friends are the family you choose' engraved on its shiny surface.

Kat swallowed the lump in her throat as she looked at them in turn.

"You will always be my favourite Americans," she said with a slight hitch in her voice. "Thanks for embracing life on the cut, my home, and me. I'll never forget you."

Hugs followed, and Kat tried to control her emotions. She couldn't blame the bump on the head this time.

"Before we kick you and Jordan out so we can all get some well-earned rest, I think we need to take a group Polaroid picture for Kat's rogues' gallery." He pulled out

Kat's camera and started herding everyone into position. It took four attempts before they got a photograph without anyone's head cut off, but the final image was perfect. Kat pressed it to her chest as she said goodnight to Ted, Martha, Beth, and Cole.

"Thank you for a fabulous evening," she said, trying to hold back more tears. "I'm so lucky to have had you all in my life, even briefly."

She walked back to the *Creaky Cauldron* with Jordan in silence, her fingers playing with the charm bracelet on her wrist and her mind still replaying the thanks and gratitude everyone had lavished on her.

"I'm not sure these Floating Solo experiences will ever be the same again," Kat said quietly as they unlocked the door and filed into the living space.

"Have we traumatised you for life?" Jordan chuckled. "Are you going to become a hermit and never allow strangers inside the hallowed walls of the *Creaky Cauldron* again?"

"Something like that," she teased back. "I love my life, but you, all of you, have shown me how much I miss having family and friends around."

"You have amazing friends, Kat. They all rallied around when you had your accident."

"Oh, I know. I don't mean I want to change my friends. I don't know what I mean, to be honest. The accident has left me thinking peculiar thoughts, so just ignore me. Near-death experiences have an effect on people all the time."

Jordan pushed a loose strand of her hair back behind

her ear, trailing his fingers down her neck. "I couldn't ignore you if I tried."

"You're leaving tomorrow," she said in a whisper. "We'll probably never see each other again."

The air was thick with anticipation as Jordan's hand slid down her arm until he was holding her hand. The soft amber glow from the lamps danced around the space, casting enchanting shadows on the walls. Her gaze dropped to his lips.

The entire day and evening had been magical, but Kat couldn't push aside the overpowering dread of watching Jordan walk away.

As if the looming finale gave her the courage she needed, she leaned forward and kissed Jordan tenderly.

"Come with me." She tugged him slowly along behind her, heading down the corridor towards her bedroom. Her heart thrashed wildly in her chest as her desire for him sent an electrical charge through her body. She felt like they were connected by a magnetic force that neither of them could resist.

Jordan pushed the bedroom door closed behind them, his expression full of longing and understanding. If tonight was their final night together, then it was going to be special.

His touch sent shivers down her spine as he unbuttoned her blouse and slid the soft material over her shoulders. Leaning in, he pressed his lips to hers in a mix of passion and tenderness.

The space between them faded, leaving only their heavy breaths and soft touches in the confines of the small bedroom.

He nuzzled her neck as she wrestled him out of his shirt, and peppered her shoulders with kisses, unhooking her bra and letting it fall to the floor with the rest of their clothes. His mouth explored her breasts, making her moan as he caught her nipple and sucked.

"I never want this night to end," he whispered between kisses.

Kat's stomach lurched at his words as his strong hands circled her waist and gently moved her to the bed. She unzipped his jeans slowly, loving his groan of anticipation.

Naked and aroused, they climbed into bed, wrapping their limbs together, kissing and touching. Jordan's square shoulders arched as she explored his hardness.

Time stood still as they lost themselves in each other, oblivious to the rocking of the boat as it moved in rhythm with their lovemaking.

Eventually, spent and satisfied, they fell asleep in each other's arms.

★ ★ ★

Kat awoke to Jordan smoothing the hair from her forehead as he kissed her softly on the lips.

"Good morning," he said with a warm smile.

The last time they slept together, he had run away, but Kat preferred waking up beside him over finding an empty bed.

"Morning."

Neither of them was in a rush to move. Kat rested her head on Jordan's chest with her arm wrapped around his waist and her leg casually resting over his. He stroked his fingers up and down her back as birds chirped beyond the window and water splashed softly against the hull.

"I don't think I'll ever forget this moment," she said, turning her face so she could kiss his lips. He responded, kissing her deeply and pulling her closer.

They made love again, but this time it was hot and fast, a feverish end to their time together, full of desire and urgency, before squeezing into the tiny shower cubicle together and laughing until their sides ached.

Jordan packed his bag as Kat readied the boat for its final cruise. The lump in her throat refused to shift as she heard him bumping around inside the boat. She had done the one thing she told Stephanie she wouldn't do. She had fallen in love with Jordan Harrington.

A jumble of thoughts crashed through her mind as she weighed up the idea of telling him how she felt and seeing what he made of it. What could they do? Did long-distance relationships really work? Would he come back to visit with Martha when she checked on her investment? Was that enough for either of them? Being close to him sucked the air from her lungs, and the thought of not being able to touch him or kiss him regularly was too much to deal with.

It was hopeless. No matter how she looked at the scenarios, there was only one outcome. She had to let him go.

What they had shared over the two weeks spent on the *Creaky Cauldron* would have a special place in her heart forever, but for her and Jordan's sanity, they needed to say a final goodbye.

As she recalled the highs and lows of their trip, tears trailed down her face, but she didn't wipe them away. She needed to let herself feel the sadness. As Stephanie had always told her, *to appreciate the good emotions, you must also embrace the uncomfortable ones*. Well, she was ready to embrace it all.

Kat stepped onto the deck and gazed out across the canal and to the horizon where the finish line waited.

"Hey Kat, is everything ready?" Beth called out to her from *Dreamcatcher*.

"We're good to go when Ted's ready," she shouted back. The idea was to let Martha steer the crew boat into the marina first so Cole could capture the *Creaky Cauldron* returning, creating the perfect circle.

They were about an hour away from their destination. An hour from the grand finale and the heartbreak Kat knew she would feel watching Jordan walk up that path to the waiting cars.

As everyone gathered on the towpath, the mood was more subdued than usual. Kat knew she didn't want the trip to end, for obvious reasons, but from the downturned mouths and sad eyes, it seemed the rest of them felt the same.

"We'll all stay in touch," Kat said, trying to lift their spirits. Returning to the marina was the final piece of the Floating Solo magic. It was usually the moment her guests knew the answers to all the questions that had driven them to book their holiday in the first place.

She had seen hundreds of light-bulb moments on this single stretch of canal, and she wanted all of her new friends to experience this too.

"Make a wish," she said finally. "Think about something you want to be, do, or have, and wish for it. The last stretch of this canal is magic, and if you can dream it, then you can become it."

Beth giggled. "Now I know why your boat is called the *Creaky Cauldron*. You're a bit of a mystic wiccan, aren't you?"

"Don't you believe in magic?" Kat asked with a smile.

Cole slid his hand into Beth's and answered Kat's question with one simple action. They had found each other on this trip and love was the greatest magic of all.

"My wish is to keep sharing the magic with others by investing in Kat's Floating Solo business," Martha said to the audible gasps of the others.

"Why didn't you tell us." Ted said as he wrapped his arm around Martha's shoulder. "This is fantastic news and a match made in heaven."

"We still have to draw up the contracts and finalise the paperwork and finances, but I felt it was the right thing to do. What Kat has created here is wonderful, and I want to be a small part of that, even from a million miles away. It's something my uncle wanted for me as well, so I feel like I'm honouring his memory."

They fell into an excited chatter about the future of Floating Solo and how many boats the fleet would have.

"Maybe I could come back to Warwickshire and help you decorate the other boats," Beth said, jumping up and down on the towpath. "It would be so much fun, and I could do you some behind-the-scenes stuff for that too."

"I'd be happy to film some promotional videos for you both," Cole added.

Kat beamed at them, nodding along with their ideas and enthusiasm to help.

Although it was Martha making the investment, it did feel like a family venture as the others shared their excitement.

"What about you, Jordan? What's your wish?" Kat looked up into his handsome face and smiled. From the conversations they had had about his career, it was looking more likely that his wishes would be granted the second he set foot back in LA. Ted had received more scripts for the lead in three potential romances, and Martha was getting emails every day asking for a meeting.

"My wish is that we never lose this." He waved his hand in a circle to encompass the entire group. "You all know what an ass I was at the start of this trip, and for that I'm sorry. But what we've built here is special, and so my wish is that our friendships last forever."

"Group hug." Beth shouted, diluting the beauty of Jordan's message somewhat but breaking the melancholy enough to make everyone laugh. She grabbed her phone and began filming around the circle like she was at the centre of a rugby scrum.

"And that's a wrap!" she said to the camera. "We've had a blast on the canal with Jordan and Kat and can't wait to share the docuseries with you. Sign up at the link below to find out more. We'll be back in LA soon, but in the meantime, thanks for watching."

Just like that, it was done. Her behind-the-scenes footage was over. Would Kat disappear into the social media wilderness again, or had Beth's videos built enough momentum for Tom to build on?

"Right then." Kat clapped her hands to rally the troops. "It's time for the big finish. Martha, if you take *Dreamcatcher* out, we'll follow behind in about half an hour and at a slower pace to give you time to set up with cameras as Jordan brings us into the marina."

"See you there," Martha said, pulling Kat into a tight hug.

She watched Martha, Ted, Cole, and Beth bound off towards the other boat and took a mental snapshot of the scene. Blake would be coming to collect *Dreamcatcher* in a few days, and she would miss not seeing it trailing behind her.

"Ready?" Jordan's soft voice pulled her away from her musings.

"Not at all," Kat replied with a sad smile. "But let's do it anyway."

Chapter Eighteen

The stretch of canal leading back to Mapleton Marina was one of Kat's favourites. The hedgerows were bursting with colour at all times of the year. It was like Mother Nature decided to plant every variety of shrub and flower so there was a constant display of her work, whether you came in the spring or the autumn.

Every so often, there would be a break in the bushes and a view would open up across the glorious Warwickshire countryside with rolling fields, terracotta roof tiles, and mighty oak trees.

To Kat, the view was like the yellow brick road leading her home.

As they cruised along the canal with *Dreamcatcher* now out of sight, she noticed the towpaths were starting to get busier. She was used to seeing multiple joggers, walkers, and dog owners, but there seemed to be more groups and families lining the waterway.

The radio crackled to life as Jordan climbed outside to join her at the tiller.

"It's a zoo up ahead," Martha's voice drifted from the handset. "The marina is packed, and the press is here too."

Kat glanced across at Jordan, who rolled his eyes. The peace and calm of life on the water was about to be shattered. If it was even the slightest bit like the paparazzi outside the hospital, then getting their relaxed return on film was going to be impossible.

"Roger that. Are we still okay to proceed?"

"Yes, Cole has set up the camera and we've got some help from the locals keeping the crowds back, but I wanted to forewarn you both."

With Jordan now standing on the stern, the groups of people gathered on the towpath began to wave and shout hello. A wall of phones followed them as they drifted past. Jordan switched easily into his celebrity role and waved back, calling out to people with an occasional 'hello' and 'thank you'.

Cruising at such a slow speed allowed the excited onlookers to engage with the pair.

When Kat heard them calling her name, she relaxed into it and started waving back too. She wondered if this was what William and Kate felt like whenever they went out in public.

"Welcome home."

"We've loved following your trip."

"Kiss her, Jordan."

"Will there be another series?"

The questions were thrown from all sides of the canal and even from the crowds that now congregated on the bridges.

Mixed in amongst the general public and their iPhones were journalists lugging their camera equipment. Kat and Jordan spotted a news van parked down a country lane running parallel to the canal with the cameraman standing on the van's roof. They waved in his direction and he nearly fell off as he waved back.

"Do you get this everywhere you go?" she asked as she smiled at a young couple who were clapping and cheering.

"It hasn't been like this for a long time," he replied. "The attention I was getting usually involved insults, a lot of profanity, and me being shepherded around between two burly bodyguards."

"Wow. I'll take the clapping and cheering any day."

Jordan laughed at her comment. "Hopefully, Ted's docuseries will change the tide, and people will start seeing me as a human being again."

"Nope, I don't think so," Kat said with a cheeky smile and a sharp shake of her head. "You'll always be a super-sexy pin-up to me. Don't get any grand ideas of being human."

He threw his head back and laughed, much to the delight of everyone on the riverbank, before wrapping his arm around Kat's shoulder. She slid her arm around his waist and giggled at the gasps and cheers from the onlookers. The sudden burst and click, click, click of the journalists' cameras startled the ducks, who squawked across the canal to settle in a quieter spot far from the madness.

The mouth of the marina was up ahead, and Kat gawped at the number of people lining the canal.

"Oh wow, this is insane," she muttered as she scanned the hundreds of bodies filling the towpaths and fields.

She grabbed the radio and alerted Martha to their arrival.

"We're coming up on the marina now. Over."

"Brace yourselves." came the response.

The marina was private land surrounded by fences and a padlocked gate that only boat owners could access. They approached with the marina on their left and the green fields rolling up behind it. In the distance, Kat could see the marina owner standing guard at the gate, flanked by Roger, Dotty, and Barbara. It looked like all the villagers of Mapleton had come down to help corral the crowds.

Tom was standing with Beth as they secured *Dreamcatcher*. Ted was already talking to the crowd of reporters and news cameras that had assembled in one spot behind the fences near the mouth of the marina.

Cole was positioned on the bend with the camera pointing in their direction.

"Are you ready to take her in?" Kat glanced up at Jordan, whose face shone with something akin to pride, or was it joy?

"I'm ready, Captain. You've taught me well."

Kat chuckled and stepped to the side to give him more room to manoeuvre the tiller, but he tugged her back and slipped his free hand around her shoulder. She slid her fingers into his and nestled against him.

"Lights, camera, action!" Jordan whispered in her ear as they both tried to act as naturally as possible for their arrival.

The sound was deafening as Jordan steered the narrowboat into the marina. Beyond the fences, cheers erupted from the waiting crowds, who had travelled to Mapleton Marina to get a glimpse of the Hollywood star. The boat drifted forward, and Jordan lined it up perfectly to the bank. Kat hopped off the side to grab the rope and secure the boat in place. She glanced around, trying to take in the chaos and crowds who were snapping photos and shouting for her to wave and smile.

Jordan took it all in his stride as he hopped off the boat and joined her to pull in the final rope. With the *Creaky Cauldron* secured, they turned as one and waved at the crowds.

Kat wasn't sure what to do next. Usually when she returned to the marina with her guests, it was a quiet affair where she thanked them for travelling with her, took the obligatory Polaroid selfie, and then sent them off up the path to the car park.

This was all incredibly surreal. She spotted Stephanie waving across at her from near the gate, but her friend's face was full of concern rather than the cheerful welcome home smile Kat had expected. Martha was huddled next to Stephanie, and it looked like she was having a full-on confrontation with someone on the other side of the fence.

Through the sea of bodies, a tall blonde with large sunglasses, tight white trousers, and a flimsy pink vest top scaled the fence and barged past Martha before breaking into a run. She was heading straight for where Kat and Jordan were standing.

"Oh, baby, I've missed you so much." The blonde threw herself at Jordan, almost knocking him into the marina, and smashed her lips to his.

Kat gasped but gathered herself quickly and clamped her mouth shut as the journalists' cameras burst into life.

Lexi Chivers was an unexpected addition to their grand finale, but with Jordan's sudden return to popularity, it wasn't surprising she wanted her boyfriend back.

"Jordan. Lexi. Are you back together?"

"What about Miss Sinclair?"

"What's the story?"

"Jordan, is this a love triangle?"

"Kat, what are your thoughts?"

The shock and subsequent pain in her chest from witnessing Jordan and Lexi's public reunion spurred Kat into action. Before she said something she would regret, she turned away from the heartbreaking scene and walked slowly to the stern. There were jobs to do whenever she arrived back at the marina, and now seemed like the perfect time to get started.

Lexi's action cancelled out all the warm and fuzzy feelings Kat had enjoyed on the final leg of the canal with Jordan. She hoped this wouldn't tarnish the joy of future trips for her. Only moments before, she was tucked into the safe embrace of Jordan's arms as they laughed and waved at the army of his fans who had come out to see them. Now she felt sick to the pit of her stomach and was trying to avoid the myriad of questions the crowds over the fence were throwing at her.

Stephanie arrived at her side just as Lexi pulled Jordan away from the boat and back towards the crowds.

"Are you okay?" she asked, ignoring the shouts from the journalists, who continued to pepper them with questions.

"They have history," Kat said, sneaking a quick glance at Jordan with an excitable Lexi hanging off him. "I get it.

Being with Jordan was epic in every possible way, but it was only temporary, and I'm okay with that."

It was a lie, and the words stuck in her throat as she said them. She was in love with Jordan Harrington, but in her head she had already let him go. How she dealt with her heart was something she had yet to work out.

"Who are you, and what have you done with my best friend?" Stephanie said, poking her in the ribs and making her laugh.

Kat jumped back onto the deck, took the key out of the ignition, slipped it into her pocket, and secured the back door.

"I admit it, I fell for him big time, but for my own sanity, I need to let him go. He helped me see that I'm not lost or broken and that I can love, work, and live on my own terms. I'll be forever grateful for that."

Deep down, she was disappointed that they didn't get a big romcom happy ever after, but she also needed to be realistic. Hollywood had invaded her life for two weeks, but now she could get back to building her business and coming back down to earth.

"I'm so proud of you," Stephanie said, pulling her into a warm hug.

As Kat stepped back onto the bank, Martha joined the girls, fury crashing off her in waves.

"I'm so sorry that *she* is here," Martha seethed, twitching her head in Jordan and Lexi's direction. "I had our big finish all planned out, and she's ruined it."

"It's fine, Martha. Let them have their big reunion. Jordan deserves a bit of happiness in his life."

Kat didn't miss the tut Martha gave her, but brushed it aside. She couldn't afford to let herself feel jealous or sad; she might as well be back in the beer garden at the King's Head throwing a glass of wine in someone's face.

"Are you coming to Roger's when you've finished here?" Stephanie asked.

"I'll try." In truth, one of Roger's bacon baps and a big mug of coffee wouldn't cure all her woes right now, but it would help, and she had missed seeing her village friends. "But if the journalists get their way, I'll still be here at dinnertime."

Stephanie and Martha walked back towards the gate, where Roger was still playing bouncer and stopping anyone from reaching the stars.

Kat couldn't tear her gaze away as Lexi ran her hands over Jordan's shoulders, cooing in his ear. What did surprise her was the lack of reciprocation in Jordan's body language. He kept moving as if avoiding her touch and trying to look behind him towards the boats.

"No comment!" Ted shouted as he sauntered back over to the *Creaky Cauldron*. "Honestly, they never stop."

Kat linked her arm through Ted's and rested her head on his shoulder.

"Thank you for everything," she said. "It's been an amazing experience."

Ted chuckled and kissed her forehead. "We'll stay in touch, and I'll make sure Martha lets you know how the editing process goes. Maybe we could invite you out to LA for the premiere."

"I'd like that." She wondered if she could request a seat

far away from Jordan and Lexi as part of her acceptance.

He wandered off to find Cole and start disassembling the camera equipment, and Kat clambered on board the *Creaky Cauldron* to watch everything from a safe distance. She felt like she was having an out-of-body experience and was watching all this happen to someone else.

Jordan had managed to wriggle out of Lexi's grip and whispered something into Martha's ear. Kat watched Martha's expression shift from frustration to sheer joy. Whatever he had said to her was clearly good news. Maybe he was also getting married and asked her to be his best woman or something. As Kat watched, it was like a ripple of energy washed over everyone at the marina. Martha called out for Beth, barking orders at anyone close enough to assist them, and between them and a few bystanders, they manhandled Lexi Chivers away from the moorings and back towards the gate.

The Netflix star tried to fight back against the swarm of onlookers, who were now physically manoeuvring her away from the marina. She hurled insults at Martha, who stood defiantly by the gate with her hands on her hips. Beth was pointing aggressively at the car park as if every stab of her finger in the air would move Lexi further away. The scene played out like one of those teen drama shows where the bully gets their comeuppance when the army of nerds turns on them.

Kat watched with fascination as Roger stepped up, unlocked the gate, and shooed the TV star away. Some of the journalists had broken free and were chasing after Lexi as she stormed off across the car park, still screaming profanities at Martha. Kat knew that Martha had no time for Lexi Chivers, but even so, everyone's combined efforts to make sure she didn't steal Jordan's limelight were awe-inspiring. If Martha put as much passion into their joint venture then Kat knew they couldn't fail.

Totally engrossed in whatever was happening, Kat didn't notice Jordan approach the boat.

"Permission to come aboard?" he said.

Kat nodded, confusion etched across her brow. "What's going on?"

"I wasn't expecting to see Lexi here today; it threw me."

"It's okay, I understand. I've done my bit to help you rebuild your reputation, so it's fine for you to get back to your old life again."

"I couldn't have done all this without you."

"It's included in the price – bed, board, and lifestyle revivals," Kat said with a sad smile. "I'm happy for you, Jordan. I'm happy for both of you."

"Both? What on earth are you talking about?"

"You and Lexi are getting back together, and your career is getting back on track. It's everything you wished for."

"No, it isn't. Lexi isn't the future I want. I hated the person I'd become when I was with her. You helped me realise that. Maybe it's that ridiculously slow pace on your canals or all this British fresh air, but what I want is standing right here in front of me."

"I don't know what to say," Kat stammered.

"How do you feel about on-screen kisses?"

She laughed as he pulled her into a tight embrace on the deck of the *Creaky Cauldron* and kissed her in full view of everyone. The excited chatter, cheers, and click of the journalists' cameras filled the air.

Pulling away briefly, Jordan whispered, "There's no need for you to float solo any more, Kat."

Epilogue

One year later

Kat pulled the door closed behind her, juggling her keys, a bunch of yellow roses, and the oversized gift bag overflowing with pink tissue paper. The drizzle and grey clouds had blown through to leave a crisp spring morning, a bright blue sky, and a watery yellow sun that made the grass sparkle.

The gravel crunched underfoot as she rushed down the path to the garden gate, stumbling briefly over her own feet. Although she had set an alarm that would have given her plenty of time to shower and get ready, she hadn't factored in a potential power cut.

While moving into the cottage on the canal was a dream come true, it was also fraught with challenges – the wiring and electrics being one of them.

St Peter's Church was only a short walk from the canal, and she could see people milling around outside. The car park was already full of townie cars, no doubt Tom's new connections from his thriving social media business. As she scanned the SUVs and sports cars, she couldn't see any chauffeur-driven Range Rovers. Perhaps Martha hadn't been able to make time to come over.

Stephanie and Tom stood at the front of the church

with the minister, their heads bent in private conversation. Kat scanned the pews. There was no Martha, no Beth or Cole, and more importantly, no Jordan.

"Where have you been?" Stephanie said in a rush, handing the baby over to Tom and pulling Kat into a tight hug. "I honestly thought you were going to miss the entire thing and I'd have to ask Barbara or Dotty to stand in as godmother."

Kat chuckled and pushed the flowers into her friend's hand, setting the gift bag on the nearest seat.

"You know I wouldn't miss this for the world. The stupid power went out again."

"Maybe living on land just isn't meant to be for you." Stephanie winked.

"I'm not going to let a run-down old cottage beat me," Kat said with a laugh. "I've survived a biblical storm and near drowning. A bit of electrical wiring is a doddle."

"Roger will know someone who can help. That man's like a walking directory."

Kat nodded absentmindedly and scanned the church once more.

"He's not here," Stephanie said, automatically tilting her head to the side in that 'I'm so sorry' way that people do. "I honestly thought he'd come."

"Me too."

Tom joined them then and leaned in to kiss Kat's cheek as the baby gurgled and smiled up at her.

"We're glad you're here, Kat."

The minister interrupted them by calling for everyone to take their seats so they could get started. Kat lowered herself onto the wooden bench next to Stephanie with a tight lump in her throat.

"Welcome to St Peter's," the minister began. "I want to extend a special welcome to baby Ava; to her parents, Stephanie and Tom; and to her godparents, Tom's sister Penny, and Tom and Stephanie's friends, Kathryn and Jordan…"

Tom coughed and made a few hand gestures towards the minister, who slid his eyes across the front pew until he reached Kat and mimicked Stephanie's tilt of the head.

If she hadn't been in church, Kat might have rolled her eyes and muttered a swearword, but instead, she smiled at the minister and urged him to carry on with a flick of her hand.

The service continued with a beautiful reading Stephanie had found about new life and the potential for love and good health, followed by an upbeat hymn that had everyone smiling and swaying. As the song came to an end Kat's phone vibrated in her pocket. Under the ever-watchful eye of the minister, she left it where it was and tried to ignore the incessant vibrations.

"I'd like to call upon the godparents to join me," the minister said once the congregation had settled back into their seats after the hymn.

Kat joined Penny by the font alongside Stephanie and Tom. She tried not to look out across the sea of faces who, no doubt, were hoping for a glance of the Hollywood action hero who should have been standing at her side.

Ava watched the minister wave his hands around as he talked about the joy of babies and the hope they hold for the future, and Kat giggled when Ava sneezed and the sound echoed through the church, making the baby jump.

The minister turned to Tom and Stephanie and addressed them. "You have asked to have your child baptised. In doing so you are accepting the responsibility…"

Kat zoned out as he continued speaking. Her mind was elsewhere, thinking about the promises Jordan had made. She had considered all the options of a long-distance relationship back on the *Creaky Cauldron* during their trip last May, but they had pushed aside any potential difficulties because they wanted to make it work.

Penny dug her elbow into Kat's ribcage, startling her out of her stupor. The minister's gaze was fixed on her as if waiting for an answer.

"I'm sorry, could you repeat the question?"

Stephanie buried her face into Ava's blanket and giggled, offering no help as to what Kat was supposed to do.

"Are you ready to help Stephanie and Tom in their duty as Christian parents?"

"Oh, right, yes, of course, no problem at all."

The congregation giggled and Kat was sure she spotted the minister roll his eyes.

Penny leaned over and whispered in Kat's ear.

"We do," they both said together.

Kat was mortified, but her distress was quickly pushed aside as the main doors of the church burst open and Jordan appeared.

There was a ripple of gasps from everyone seated as Jordan Harrington rushed up the aisle to where they stood.

"I'm so sorry we're late," he gushed in his thick American accent. "The connecting flight got delayed."

Kat caught sight of Martha, Beth, and Cole slide into one of the pews at the back of the church and grinned at them.

Jordan pulled Stephanie into a big bear hug, tickling Ava's chin as he did, and then shook Tom's hand. Penny's mouth hung slightly wide as Jordan winked at her as he manoeuvred his way to where Kat was standing.

"Sorry, big guy," he said to the minister. "One godfather present and correct."

Kat lowered her head to hide the ridiculous smile that now spread across her face.

"Thank you, Mr Harrington. Let us continue." The minister handled the chaos with grace, and before long, he was reaching his arms to the ceiling and finishing with "Bless you."

They all filed out into the sunshine, where Kat's American friends immediately surrounded her.

"It's so good to see you all," she gushed. Although they had only spent a couple of weeks together, this small Floating Solo group had become family to her.

"We've missed you," Beth squealed, pulling her phone from her back pocket and jumping straight in for a video. "Look who I'm with, guys. Yes, we're back in the UK visiting our favourite narrowboat captain."

Kat waved at the camera. It didn't feel quite so strange doing silly videos with Beth after spending so much time creating their behind-the-scenes shots last year. It was thanks to those short, snappy videos that her Floating Solo business had exploded, Jordan's career was back on track, and Ted's docuseries was involved in a bidding war for the rights to air it.

Stephanie sauntered over with a happy Ava on her arm and Beth shot off for cuddles, closely followed by Cole. It warmed Kat's heart to see that the two of them were still going strong.

As she watched Beth cooing over the baby, two strong arms circled her waist from behind.

"I understand the godfather at these events usually goes home with the godmother," Jordan whispered into her ear.

"I believe that perk only applies to the best man and chief bridesmaid at a wedding, but nice try."

She laughed as he whirled her around and cupped her face in his hands.

"I've missed you," he said, leaning in to kiss her tenderly.

"I've missed this," Kat breathed as she pulled him in closer and kissed him back.

Kat pushed open the cottage window and called out to Jordan and Cole, who were busy painting the small fence that edged the garden. The canal glistened behind them.

"Lunch is ready."

They waved at her and began clearing away the pots of paint.

"There's so much to do around here, and getting the boys to finish off odd jobs whenever we are back in the UK is going to take forever," Beth said as she put the salad bowl and platter of sandwiches on the table. "Don't you miss living on the *Creaky Cauldron*?"

"Sometimes. Especially when I have a power cut or the roof leaks, but having a home on land is something I always wanted. It's easier to run a growing business from here too. The fact that Jordan and you guys can only visit once every few months is hard, but we'll make it work. It means I get to focus on running Floating Solo."

"How is the business doing?"

"We've got five boats in the fleet now," Martha jumped in, a smile lighting up her face. "With two more potentials in the North."

"Anyone would think you enjoyed being Kat's business partner," Jordan said as he walked inside and planted an affectionate kiss on the top of Martha's head.

"I adore it," she said with a laugh and a clap of her hands. Although she had recently celebrated her sixty-fifth birthday, Martha was like an excitable schoolgirl at that moment. "And Kat is the best business partner anyone could wish for. The fleet is fully booked for months to come, and we are ahead of our sales projections for the year."

They spoke more about the plans for Floating Solo, the state of the cottage and what Kat hoped to do to the place, and the scripts Martha was receiving for Jordan.

As Kat nursed her cup of coffee she glanced around the table at her new family. Martha had become more than a business partner; although she had intended to be a silent partner, she had been able to split her time between LA and the UK to give Kat as much support as she could. Between them, they bought the right boats, kitted them out to Kat's *Creaky Cauldron* standard, and launched a new range of holidays, from weekend jaunts to fortnight trips.

Cole interrupted her thoughts by standing up and saying, "I have an announcement!"

They all looked up at him expectantly.

"As you know, Beth and I have been seeing each other for a year now and things have been going well. I wanted to tell you… Well, *we* wanted to tell you that I've given up my apartment in LA and we're moving in together. We've put a deposit on a place near Santa Monica and we get the keys for it in a few weeks."

Everyone started congratulating them both. Beth's smile lit up the room as she pulled out her phone and started showing them pictures of their new home.

"I'm so happy for you both," Kat said, hugging Beth and feeling like a big sister who had watched her sibling grow up overnight.

"If it wasn't for you, Kat, we might never have gotten together. I'll be forever grateful to you and your solo holiday adventures."

"As Stephanie would say, the magic of the *Creaky Cauldron* strikes again."

They swapped coffee for a bottle of Prosecco Kat found in the fridge and toasted to happiness, new adventures, and settling down, or growing up as Cole called it.

That night when she climbed into bed her heart was full.

"I didn't think it was possible to feel this happy," she said softly as Jordan gathered her in his arms. "My best friends have a gorgeous daughter, my business is booming, and my other friends are moving in together. This has been a magical weekend."

Jordan didn't answer; instead he made a slight huff sound and Kat twisted her body so she was facing him. His handsome face was illuminated in the moonlight streaming through the cottage window, and she pushed his hair out of his eyes as she leaned in to kiss him.

"What's the matter?" Her heart jumped a little as if preparing itself for bad news.

"I don't think I can keep doing the odd long weekend here and there, Kat. It's too hard."

She dropped her hand from his face, trying to keep the feeling of devastation from her expression. Surely she couldn't feel so happy one moment and then be crushed yet again the next.

"What does that mean?" She was asking the question, but she wasn't sure she wanted to hear his answer.

"It means I can't keep running backwards and forwards. I need more stability in my life. You understand that, don't you?"

"Of course I do. Stability is the one thing I've always craved."

"Exactly, that's why I knew you'd understand. Will you help me tell Martha?"

Kat felt like she had drifted off and missed their entire conversation.

What did she understand? What did Jordan need to tell Martha?

"How can *I* help? I'm not sure I understand what you're saying myself."

Jordan brushed his hand along her cheek and pulled her in for a kiss. It began softly but intensified as he swept his hand over her shoulder and down to her waist.

Kat's head began to swim and she pushed away from him, breathing heavily.

"Jordan, stop it. Are you breaking up with me?"

His eyes widened and he let out a small gasp. "Why would you think that?"

"You've just said you can't do the long weekends here and there and need stability. I get it, we knew a long-distance relationship would be challenging, but I thought we were doing okay."

"We're doing more than okay, Kat. I don't want to be running back to LA all the time. I want to live here, with you."

Kat let his words sink in for a moment, not quite believing what she was hearing.

"You don't want to go home?"

Jordan smiled that Hollywood smile which stopped people in their tracks. She had seen it happen firsthand, and now here he was giving her that exact smile. "You are my home, Kat. I want to stay here in this battered old cottage and build a life together with you."

His words melted something deep inside her chest and she gasped.

"What? How?"

"I'd live here and travel for work. It's simple, but it means I'd come back home to you here when shooting finished."

"You would give up your LA life to live in a run-down cottage on the banks of a canal in Warwickshire?" If Ted were here right now he would be noting all this down as an idea for one of his films. It felt like the storyline of a Hallmark Christmas movie.

"I don't mind where we live. We could be back on the *Creaky Cauldron* for all I care. I just know that home is wherever you are. I love you, Kathryn Sinclair. I think I loved you the moment you shouted at me on the riverbank and called me a stuck-up idiot."

Kat laughed but didn't have a chance to reply as Jordan kissed her again. His kisses were soft and warm, and she melted into him as he wrapped his arms around her.

She had everything she could ever want. Her quaint little cottage, a fleet of boats and a thriving business, great friends, and a man she loved and who loved her back. There was nothing else she wanted or needed in the world.

Jordan pulled back slightly so he could gaze down at her. He tucked her hair behind her ear and kissed the end of her nose.

"Marry me," he whispered.

Acknowledgements

To my amazing kids and parents, who always have my back.

A huge thank you to Sooz for believing in my story and helping me make it better – once you had recovered from the shock of me writing a romance, of course! You are the most dedicated editor a girl could wish for.

To Holly, Gav, and Liliput for confirming my love of narrowboats and a huge thanks to Paul Smith for sharing all his knowledge of living on the cut and taking us on an amazing discovery day.

To my incredible readers who turn the pages of my books – without you, I wouldn't be able to do what I do. Thank you for your support, excitement, and engagement.

To Jen for helping me bring this book to life, and to Claire for the fabulous cover design.

About the Author

S helley Wilson is a word nerd with a passion for storytelling and a mission to inspire and entertain. She is an English multi-genre author of romance, historical fiction, YA fiction, and motivational self-help titles.

She lives in a leafy suburb in the West Midlands, UK with her three children and a spoilt black cat called Luna. Shelley is a solo traveller, searching for stories and inspiration in her VW campervan called Snoopy, and is obsessed with exploring castles and researching anything mythological, supernatural, or historical.

When she's not writing, she enjoys reading, travelling, dancing around her kitchen, and rewatching old shows.

https://linktr.ee/ShelleyWilson72

Also by Shelley Wilson

The Last Princess
Hood Academy
The Phantom's Curse

THE GUARDIANS SERIES
Guardians of the Dead
Guardians of the Sky
Guardians of the Lost Lands

THE IMMORTALS SERIES
Blood Born
Blood Torn

NON-FICTION TITLES
How I Changed My Life in a Year
How I Motivated Myself to Succeed
Motivate Me! Oracle Guidebook
Meditation for Children
Meditation for Tweens and Teens
Self-Help for the Helpless

Printed in Great Britain
by Amazon

51477178R00158